*"Perhaps I should introduce myself.
I am the Earl of Templecombe,"*

the curricle's driver said, his voice devoid of sympathy.
"I am well-known for careless manners, but even I can
hardly let you ride home with a sprained ankle. Headley
shall catch your horse, but he, not you, will ride it home.
I cannot leave a maiden in distress, even one clad in
masculine clothing. It is a great bore, but there it is."

In one quick move, Lord Templecombe took the
girl in his arms and flung her up onto the curricle's
high seat by the driver's place. He had taken
charge of her as though he intended to do so
henceforward . . .

Novels By Caroline Courtney

Duchess in Disguise
A Wager For Love
Love Unmasked
Guardian of The Heart

Published By
WARNER BOOKS

CAROLINE COURTNEY

Dangerous Engagement

WARNER BOOKS

A Warner Communications Company

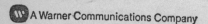

1

A huge black stallion was galloping down the grassy verge of the country lane. Its hooves pounded the turf, scattering bits of grass and earth against the hedges. Its glossy mane flew back in the wind made by its reckless speed. On its back crouched a slim figure, urging it on with cries of encouragement. The rider was so small and slight that it might almost have been a child. The boyish figure was clad in riding breeches and boots, but no hat. Instead, tangled curls as black as the stallion's glossy coat flew in the wind.

"Come on, Diabolo," shouted the rider. The voice was that of a girl. At closer inspection a bystander might have noticed that the mass of tumbled locks framed a delicate face, in which dark eyes blazed with excitement. Under its rider's encouragement, the powerful steed quickened its pace. Then with a frantic effort, the girl pulled at the reins. The big horse responded, suddenly breaking out of its gallop to come to a shuddering halt. Only superhuman riding skill could have achieved that startlingly abrupt stop.

Round the corner, at an equally breakneck speed,

there appeared a racing curricle. The frail-looking, high-perched two-wheeler was pulled by two perfectly matched grays either side of the pole. It was going flat out, but its driver, conscious at the last minute of the horse and rider on the verge of the narrow lane, gave a flick of his whip to the pair. With a reckless sway of the vehicle's whole body, they swung out of the way just in the nick of time, coming to a sudden halt just ten yards down the road.

From the seat at the back of the curricle jumped a groom, who ran to hold the heads of the two sweating and stamping horses. Flecks of foam dropped to the muddy road as the pair champed at their bits with nervous excitement.

On the green verge, the slim young rider was having difficulties with her powerful steed, which had caught the grays' nervousness. Diabolo was plunging and rearing. "Quiet, Diabolo," she murmured, gently patting its damp neck, calming the frantic beast with soothing talk.

"What the devil do you think you were doing, boy." The harsh tones came from the curricle's driver, a tall, powerful-shouldered man. He had his horses well under control by now, but the same could not be said for his temper. He was scowling with ill-concealed rage.

Casting a hasty glance at him while she tried to keep her stallion quietened, the girl could see that he was no ordinary traveler. His many-caped greatcoat had the immaculate air of a garment that could only have come from a London tailor. His high-crowned beaver hat was set at exactly the right angle. Everything about him bespoke the careless nobleman, and a nobleman in a very bad temper. The aquiline features were glowering with anger. But if he thought to daunt the stallion's rider with his black looks, he was mistaken. The big horse was now under control, standing still though still shivering slightly despite his rider's soothing hand.

"What the devil were *you* doing?" was the fiery reply. "You were driving like a madman. If I had not heard you coming, we might easily have had a serious accident. Had you no thought that others, beside yourself, might be using the road?"

"Whippersnappers like yourself, boy, should be polite to their betters," he snapped back, obviously under the mistaken impression that he had encountered a schoolboy on leave from his lessons. "Go back to your books, boy, and leave the roads for gentlemen."

"Are you usually so rude to ladies?" came the reply. The slim girl on the horse continued to pat its trembling flanks, but her voice was icy with anger. "You forget your manners. I am Miss Melbury, and this lane goes through my land."

The driver in the curricle gave a stiff bow, and lifted his hat a little way. "I cannot be expected to recognize a lady who is so lost to all propriety that she wears boy's clothing. Where is your accompanying groom, Miss Melbury? Tell me, do you normally show so little regard to convention?"

The slim figure sat defiantly upright. Even her posture, astride the big horse, was an affront to convention, but she did not seem to care. Only a telltale flush spread over her cheeks. "I do not have to be insulted by strangers upon the public highway," she said coldly, gathering up her reins. "You are right, sir; the presence of a groom might have spared me the insults you have offered. I do not know who you are, but I can only advise you to show more care in the future. This road is quite often used by local people, and even you must admit that to kill an innocent bystander might be—what shall I say?—*inconvenient*."

The words were hardly out of her mouth when round the corner from the same direction as that of the curricle, came a small country cart filled with cabbages and drawn by a donkey. The shaggy beast took one look at the obstructions in its path, stopped dead, and let out an earth-shattering bray.

It was too much for the gray horses, who reared up in fright. The groom at their head hung on with white knuckles, and the driver, with consummate skill, caught their mouths with the reins. With a struggle that would have defeated a lesser whip he kept the high-spirited pair under control.

But their panic had affected the black stallion. Frantic with fear, he tore the reins from the control of his slim rider, and bolted down the road. The girl on his back could do little more than cling to the saddle and stick on the terrified animal. They disappeared from sight round the bend of the road.

"Come, Headley, we'll be going on," was all the driver said.

"Yes, my lord. We'll be late as it is for the race meeting," was the groom's reply, as he let go of the horses' heads and ran around to his seat at the back of the curricle.

Just as the grays were about to spring forward, there was a distinct noise of a cry from the direction taken by the bolting horse. "Damn," swore the driver, holding his pair in hand with difficulty.

For a moment he hesitated as if undecided, but an intervention came from an unexpected source. The donkey cart was being led by an old man. "My lord," came his quavering voice, " 'tis Miss Miranda in trouble. Likely she will need your aid."

Muttering something, undoubtedly uncomplimentary, under his breath, the driver sighed. "Right, Headley," he said in a resigned tone. "We cannot leave Miss Melbury to her fate. I shall turn the horses around, and we will go and rescue her."

With astonishing skill, he turned the sweating restive horses round in the roadside—a maneuver that would have taxed all the expertise of a first-class coachman. At a brisk trot they set off down the road, followed slowly by the recalcitrant ass and its elderly companion.

About two hundred yards down the lane, the curricle came upon the scene of what was obviously an accident. A four-bar gate led from the road into a meadow. On its far side was the crumpled boyish figure. A little farther in the field was the black thoroughbred, grazing quietly, as if nothing could disturb his new-found serenity.

"Well, Miss Melbury, you are well served for your recklessness," said the curricle's driver, as he stopped his horses. The groom ran to their heads, and the driver dismounted from the frail vehicle to investigate the accident.

From the other side of the gate there was silence at first. The girl, in her shocking male attire, seemed to be struggling to hold back feminine fears. With difficulty she raised herself to look up at her rescuer, supporting herself with one arm. It was clear from the way she had fallen, with one leg bent at an odd angle beneath her body, that she must have suffered some kind of injury. After a moment or two, she managed to say in a voice which showed no sound of trembling, "I think I must have sprained my ankle."

Opening the gate, the curricle's driver went over to her. "If I lend you my arm, can you rise?" he asked in tones devoid of sympathy.

Biting her lips, the girl clutched at his arm. With difficulty she raised herself to a standing position, but when she tried to take a step forward, it was too much. She gave a smothered gasp and turned chalk white. Her rescuer grabbed at her swaying form. "Don't spoil it all, Miss Melbury," he said in an amused tone of voice. "Don't swoon on me like a fashionable Miss. I had expected tougher behavior from an Amazon who rides at your outrageous pace."

His mocking words acted like magic on the girl. She pulled herself together, and with a creditable pretense at not feeling pain, limped toward the curricle. As soon as she could she let go of her helper's arm, and supported herself by leaning on the curricle side.

"If your groom can catch Diabolo for me, I shall be quite all right, sir," she gasped. "I am not in the habit of falling at four-bar gates. I lost my stirrups when Diabolo bolted. Otherwise I assure you I can take such obstacles in my stride."

"Perhaps I should introduce myself. I am the Earl of Templecombe," was the smooth reply. "I am well known for my careless manners, but even I can hardly let you ride home in such a plight with a sprained ankle. Headley shall catch Diabolo, as you call him, but he, not you, will ride it home. I cannot leave a maiden in distress, even one clad in masculine clothing. It is a great bore, but there it is."

For a moment it looked as if Miranda Melbury would take offense at the rude way the offer of help was put, but a spasm of pain caught her. Leaning against the curricle, she could only manage the words "I am most grateful, Lord Templecombe." With an ineffectual gesture, she tried to climb up onto the high sporting vehicle, but only succeeded in causing herself further pain. Once again she went white and had to lean heavily against the curricle in order to stay upright.

"Come, Miss Melbury. Let me help you." Though the words were respectful, the action that accompanied them was not. In one quick move, Lord Templecombe took the girl in his arms, and flung her up onto the curricle's high seat by the driver's place. "Headley," he ordered, "I shall leave you here. Catch the stallion and bring it on after us. Where do you live, fair Amazon?"

"Melbury Place" was the cool reply. Uncomfortably perched on the high seat of the racing vehicle, Miss Melbury attempted to match Lord Templecombe's unconcerned tone. But when he climbed up beside her, she could not stop a blush stealing onto her cheeks. "It is most kind of you, Lord Templecombe," she said with a gallant attempt at a cool tone. "But I do not know whether I should drive beside you, without a groom as a chaperon."

"Such scruples are rather out of place, Miss Melbury," was the earl's reply. "The impropriety of driving with me without a groom is nothing compared with the shocking fact that you are wearing boy's clothes. You are a hoyden, Miss Melbury, and what is more you are most unsuitably mounted. That stallion is far too strong for a slip of a girl like yourself."

"I have had Diabolo since he was a foal." Miranda Melbury began to lose her temper. "He is as gentle as a lamb, and besides, I broke him myself. If it hadn't been for that wretched donkey, not to mention your absurdly fast driving, nothing would have been amiss. It was an unfortunate accident, nothing more, and the most experienced rider might have fallen off. What is more, you know it."

The curricle had been proceeding down the lane at a pace as fast as its earlier one, as she spoke these words. With a sudden gesture, its driver pulled up the two horses. Without a word, he took the reins in his right hand, and with his left pulled the girl at his side toward him. His strength was remarkable, and she could not pull out of his reach.

She found herself staring into cool gray eyes which were full of amusement. To her horror they came closer, as the earl coolly and calmly kissed her full on the lips. As he took his mouth away, he murmured: "Such sweet lips, and yet such a very sour temper. Miss Melbury, you are a firebrand who needs somebody to break you in, like you broke your stallion."

As he released his grasp, turned to his horses and spurred them on, Miranda struggled desperately with her scattered senses. For a moment she felt . . . she did not know exactly what. Then after stunned disbelief, her mood turned to one of rage. Without thinking of the horses or her own safety, she turned round to the man at her side and slapped his smiling face.

With a horrifying jerk, the two gray horses leaped out of control, as the earl, without meaning to, slackened his grasp on the reins. The curricle swayed dangerously, and without realizing it, Miranda found herself clutching at the very man whose face she had just slapped.

"Little fool!" he shouted, but that was all. His whole attention was focused on trying to regain control of the plunging horses, as they galloped at a terrifying pace down the winding country lane. For a full five minutes he fought with all his strength and attention. Finally the horses calmed down into a regular canter instead of the wild gallop, and he had time to glance at his fair companion. "Just who are you, Miss Melbury?" he said in a puzzled tone of voice.

"I am Miranda Melbury of Melbury Place," was the answer, "and my father was Sir Peter Melbury. You are strangely ignorant, Lord Templecombe. My family is well-known in this area. You probably know my aunt, Lady Eversley." As she spoke, she could not help noticing the red mark that burned on his cheek, where her hand had hit him.

"I know Lady Eversley well, and I have the greatest affection for her," was the reply. "Well, well, so you come from a respectable family and must be presumed to be a respectable girl. I don't have much time for well-brought-up young ladies, and I have not heard of you, Miss Melbury."

"I have not come out yet," she said, a hint of an apology in her voice. "But then I am not surprised you don't have much time for well-brought-up young ladies. If your behavior to women is always like this, I imagine that the only ladies who will put up with it are of a very different sort."

The driver gave a snort of laughter at her retort. "I should warn you, Miss Melbury, that if you make that sort of remark, your come-out will not be a great success. A girl like you is not supposed to know of the existence of such women."

For a moment Miranda was not sure what to say. The conversation was leading her well out of her depth. "My circle of friends, and what I may know or not know, are nothing to do with you, Lord Templecombe," she achieved, but even to her own ears it sounded rather childish. "Besides, you are losing the way. Melbury Place is to the left." The benefit of her grown-up voice was lost on her companion, as the curricle swung at the last minute through a dangerous angle toward the left. They passed through the gates of Melbury Place with barely an inch to spare in either direction at what seemed to Miranda a perilous speed. "Oh, do be careful," she could not help gasping.

The Earl of Templecombe gave a smothered chuckle, then pulled in his horses in front of the steps to the door of Melbury Place. "I can't escort you in, Miss Melbury," was all he said. "I am in a devil of a hurry, and thanks to you I am late enough already. I shall have missed the first three rounds, I should think."

"Oh, so you are going to a prize fight. How vulgar." Miranda shuddered theatrically, as if shocked. Just then the butler, who had opened the door at the sound of the cantering hooves on the driveway, came to the side of the curricle. With the help of the first footman, she climbed down. There was no more to be said, she thought. She inclined her head to the still-grinning man in the curricle.

"Will you stop for some refreshments, sir," said Sellers, the butler, without batting an eyelid at his mistress's strange arrival. Years of service with the Melbury family had given Sellers the ability not to show surprise at any odd behavior. Sir Peter Melbury had led an energetic life, which meant odd arrivals at almost any moment.

"Thank you, I am in a hurry to be off," said the earl, and without more ado he began to turn the horses. Miranda had to admire his skill with the reins, as he accomplished this delicate maneuver. At the same time Headley, his groom, arrived with the stallion. The horse had been sweating and from the look on the groom's face it had not been an uneventful ride. He slid off its back, handing the reins to a disapproving groom who had come running from the stables.

With an abrupt gesture, his master signaled for him to climb onto the back seat of the curricle, and with a sigh of relief he did so. Barely pausing to negotiate the gates, the team swung out of Melbury Place back into the road at its usual frightening speed, churning up the gravel of the driveway in its departure.

Miranda Melbury watched them leave with a strong feeling of ill will. She thought she had never before met such a rude man, nor one of such eccentric habits. It was surely very odd of a complete stranger to kiss a girl he had met in such casual circumstances.

Odd that he should have wanted to, thought Miranda. Surely not all gentlemen had this weird habit. Sir Peter, a widower of many years, had certainly never shown such tendencies. "What a strange man," she murmured, for a moment forgetting the presence of the butler and the groom. Then a thought struck her—she should have been shocked to the core of her being. Kisses like that were not things to be wondered at. She should hate the very thought of it. Do I? she asked herself.

The groom, holding the reins of Diabolo, broke into her reverie. "I reckon you gave that there groom an uneasy ride," he said, chuckling, to the horse. Then turning to Miranda, he said, " 'Tis only you that Diabolo lets on his back, Miss Miranda. You should have warned the man."

"I forgot," said Miranda absentmindedly, her

thoughts still on the odd encounter in the curricle. "Oh, the devil," she swore suddenly. She had unwarily taken a step, forgetting that her sprained ankle would pain her so. "Sorry," she apologized to the butler and the groom. "I should not have sworn like that."

Both smiled at her with the familiarity of old family servants. "You are a thorough tomboy," said Helmslow the groom. "Never you mind, Miss Miranda. You get yourself seen to, while I look after Diabolo. He needs a good groom-down, if he is not to sweat all day from this."

With a small sigh, leaning heavily on the fatherly Sellers, Miranda turned back to the house. A small figure wearing a white cap on her head and a motherly apron was waiting for her.

Nanny, an aging household power, was now the mainstay of Miranda Melbury's life. For only two months before what Miranda later christened her "escapade with an earl," her father, Sir Peter Melbury, had broken his neck out hunting. He had left behind him a very handsome fortune and estate for his only daughter, and a household of retainers like Sellers the butler, and Helmslow the head groom, who were devoted to the only Melbury left, Miranda. And, of course, to look after and cherish his only daughter there was Nanny. Nanny had been Miranda's best friend for most of her life. Lady Melbury had died young, and her daughter had therefore been brought up without a mother. But not without a mother's care. Nanny had provided that.

The widowed Sir Peter had been of a retiring nature. He had been mainly concerned with country pursuits, rarely venturing up to town, content to spend his time with his hounds, his horses, and all the sports from hunting to ratting that the countryside could afford him.

The result was that Miranda had been brought up without any insight into the fashionable world of polite society. "Time enough to think of that when you're older, puss," her father had said, stroking her cheek as he was wont to do when feeling affectionate toward his little daughter. "Won't have a daughter of mine brought up to be just a simpering Miss. Ride straight, take your fences at a steady pace, and don't cook your horses. That's what I have taught you to do. Time enough for the rest when you are older."

Miranda had enthusiastically learned her father's lessons. From the age of five, when she had been found trying to saddle up and ride one of his wildest hunters, she had been frankly horse mad. By the age of seventeen, which she now was, there was nothing in the stables too large, too wild, or too bad-tempered for her to ride.

Sir Peter had encouraged her horsy interests in every way. Taking no notice of the advice tendered to him by the staid matrons of the surrounding county, he had allowed Miranda to ride astride, wearing boy's clothing. He had insisted, of course, that she should master the art of riding side-saddle. But the heavy skirts of the traditional riding habit irked his daughter, and he sympathized with her irritation with them. The hunting season might find her out with the field, dressed in ladylike skirts and riding side-saddle in a very dashing way as she soared over the fences. Indeed, she displayed a pretty courage, as she tackled the stone walls, gates, and ditches in her path. But for ordinary hacking round the estate, and even farther afield round the immediate neighborhood, Miranda was allowed to cast aside her skirts in favor of breeches. Indeed, she would go farther. Though a groom to accompany one was the rule for any lady of quality, it was a rule Miranda would often break. Unchaperoned as she was, she had never before had any troubles, since she and her father were well-known in the locality.

The county matrons might shake their heads and whisper about Sir Peter's tomboyish daughter, but they rarely voiced their opinions out loud to his face. Some of them were too fair to blame the daughter for the shocking freedom which had, after all, been allowed by the parent. Others, who might have turned the cold shoulder on Miranda, were aware that she would be a considerable heiress. What would be shocking in an ordinary young girl might be overlooked in a young woman of wealth and independence. Besides, all the ladies agreed, Miranda would lose her hoydenish tricks once she was exposed to the polite world of London society. What the child really needed, some of the spinsters were heard to say, was a mother's loving eye. If only Sir Peter would marry again . . .

But Sir Peter declined to oblige them, though many a maiden lady had sewn extra lace on her gown for his benefit. Slowly the hopes, that had run high at the death of his young wife, began to disappear. The tragedy had broken his heart, it was rumored. Miranda, never having known her mother, was of the opinion that her father found most of the well-brought-up ladies in the neighborhood a dead bore. It was this, she privately considered, rather than a broken heart, which had stopped his entering into matrimony for a second time.

"Can't abide chattering women," he would say to his daughter as they took their daily morning ride together. "Not a brain among them. No spirit at all. Like my sister, Dorothy. She wanted to bring you up, herself. To be a parlor Miss, I've no doubt. I told her I would bring up my own daughter, thank 'ee. Nice of her to offer, of course, when your mother died. But I wasn't having any daughter of mine being brought up to be a fashionable fribble."

That same sister, Lady Dorothy Eversley, in pursuit of her duty as an aunt, had visited Melbury Place several times, and each time remonstrated with her brother about the way Miranda was being brought up. "You must get a governess for the child, Peter. Why, it's shocking to let her grow up in ignorance," had been one of her milder efforts.

"Nonsense," her brother had replied. "The child picks up all she needs from the library. The parson's teaching her Latin and Greek. She can translate Horace already, which I'll wager is more than you could do at any age, Dorothy."

"It's not the same," wailed his sister. "What about drawing and painting and the piano? It's no good teaching the child Latin and Greek, Peter, when what she needs is the polite accomplishments. Education is just no substitute."

"Stuff, Dorothy," was all Sir Peter would say. "The girl's got a sound knowledge of the classics and the best seat in the county. What else does she need?" And so the governess was never hired.

After several visits, Lady Dorothy Eversley had given up the unequal struggle. True, she kept on the best terms with Miranda, knowing that the child could not be blamed for her deplorably eccentric upbringing. She gave her exquisitely fashionable trifles for Christmas, perhaps in the hope of awakening an interest in fashion in Miranda, and she regularly sent her copies of the latest fashion plates in *La Belle Assemblée*.

But then Lord Eversley, the peer she had married,

died of a heart attack, and Lady Eversley was naturally preoccupied with the event. Though *La Belle Assemblée* regularly arrived, her visits fell off and her contact with Miranda became limited to Christmas gifts and the occasional letter.

So it was with surprise that Miranda learned that her aunt had been in touch with Nanny. "Why should she write to you, Nanny?" she asked, as the white-capped ruler of the nursery tucked her up in bed. "I know that I haven't answered her letter of sympathy about Papa's death, but I thought she had been rather thoughtless by not coming down to attend the funeral."

Miranda's sprained ankle still pained her, and dear Dr. Pye, the local practitioner who had been called in to deal with it, had recommended rest. "Not that I think you'll stay in bed more than a day or two, Miss Miranda," he had said, after recalling the many injuries he had dealt with for her, including a broken collarbone, which she had gained out hunting. "I have not forgotten how you insisted on going out with hounds with your shoulder strapped up. Foolish of Sir Peter to allow it. But, there, he was a good man."

Lady Eversley had not attended the funeral, having written an oddly phrased note which Miranda had not yet answered. She had been hurt by her aunt's non-attendance. And now Aunt Dorothy had written to Nanny, not to her.

"Now, Miss Miranda," said Nanny warningly. "Don't you fret yourself. What else should your father's sister do but write to the only person in the world who has charge of you? And that is me, for all that solicitor Mr. Scrimgeour says he is your trustee. And a very proper, kind letter it is, too. The Lord knows that I thought

20

she should have done something sooner, and come down for the funeral. But least said, soonest mended. She is doing her duty now."

"What is all this, Nanny?" said Miranda from the bed. "What is the letter *about*?"

"It is an invitation for you to make your home with her in London and come out in society What else should it be?" said Nanny firmly. "And a very good thing, too, Miss Miranda. 'Tis time you became a young lady, instead of the scamp you are now. Sweet seventeen is what you are, and you are still riding round like a boy and getting up to pranks as if you were still in the nursery."

Miranda took no notice of Nanny's scolding. It was an affectionate habit of hers to scold. Lying back on her pillows, Miranda didn't know whether to greet the news of the letter with laughter or tears. Live with Lady Eversley? Leave dear Melbury Place, and Sellers and Nanny to go and live in the smoky confines of the town? And yet what else was there for her to do? She knew she could not stay at home, with no female relative living with her, and no chaperone. Mr. Scrimegeour, her trustee, had told her as much.

"It will be a marvelous chance for you, pet," said Nanny encouragingly. "And you can't stay here, much as I would love you to. Well, it's either that or some gentrified, perked-up lady chaperone, and that I wouldn't like to see nor would you, my dear."

As Miranda lay silent, Nanny rambled on. "Mr. Sellers said, when I told him—not that his opinion is worth anything—but he said like me that it was not proper you being here without some lady in the household. There's not a servant in the house wouldn't do anything for you, if they could, but it's not fitting for a young lady to be all on her own. What Sir Peter was thinking of, leaving you all alone, without a proper guardian and only Mr. Scrimgeour, the solicitor, for a trustee, I'll never know. And your money all tied out, so that you can't barely get enough for your own wants, until you get betrothed. Well, it's a proper muddle, as I told Mr. Scrimgeour, himself. 'The way the money's been left,' I said to him, 'is enough to make a girl go out and get engaged to be married just in order to claim her own.'"

"Oh Nanny dear, do stop going on about it," said a voice from the pillows. Miranda gave a big sigh. "I want to think. If only all my money hadn't been tied up in that boring trust, I could have done just what I liked and stayed here and bred horses and hunted. But I can't get anything for the horses out of Mr. Scrimgeour, and all he allows me is pocket money. As if getting betrothed to somebody would make such a difference! I can't think what Papa had in mind."

"'Tis likely enough he was thinking of how you're such a tomboy, Miss Miranda," broke in Nanny. "Here's a chance of your life to go to London and meet all the beaux in high society and what do you talk about—breeding horses and hunting. I told your father many a time. I said to him, 'Sir Peter, that girl's being brought up to think of nothing but horses. It's not right, and it's not proper.' But would he listen? All he cared about was you, and his horses, and the time you broke your collarbone, I swear he was more concerned about whether Diabolo had sprained its fetlock than his very own daughter."

"Dear Papa. I did so love him." Tears swam into Miranda's eyes as the incident came back to her memory. "You are right, Nanny. He always taught me to think of the horses first, and myself second. I just wish he'd left me enough money so that I needn't have bothered about going to London. Why on earth did he want me to get betrothed? I don't want to marry, but now I suppose I shall have to."

"Well, my dear, it's only natural that you should get married, and perhaps that is why Sir Peter left the money in such a way. It's not right for a woman to live alone, unless she's a widow like Lady Eversley." Nanny had nearly rambled her way into criticizing the very person that she wished Miranda to live with. "You need a husband, Miss Miranda, and that's what your aunt will be able to find for you. And what I say is that you need somebody to keep a rein on you. I never could, nor Sir Peter, though he didn't try. You're as headstrong as that there stallion of yours."

"Oh, Nanny, how is Diabolo?" Miranda sat bolt upright in the large bed. "I must go down and see that he has not suffered." She flung herself out of the bed and began throwing on the clothes that lay in a neat heap on the nearby chair. Disregarding protests from her nurse, she said, "Come on, Nanny. My ankle's not hurting anymore. Anyway, I can't stay in bed all day. I should die of boredom."

Muttering her disapproval, the old woman helped her on with her clothes. Miranda put aside the breeches, and instead chose a plain day dress in a sober gray muslin. "Not that old dress, Miss Miranda," said her nurse with dismay.

"I know my aunt wouldn't like it, but I do," retorted Miranda. "Besides it's just what I need for the stables, much better than my more expensive dresses. By the way, when am I to go to my aunt?"

"At the end of the week is what she suggested, Miss Miranda."

"Oh, what a bore. I shall miss the last week of hunting. And Diabolo was going so well. Still, if I ride him on Wednesday at Brackmore Gate, I can get in one last day on Friday. They're drawing Moretom copse, and hounds always find there."

Placing a battered straw hat on her head, she paused unself-consciously in front of the mirror, not to admire herself, but as a thought suddenly struck her. "Who's going to look after things at Melbury Place, Nanny?"

"Mr. Scrimgeour thinks it best if me and Mr. Sellers are left in charge."

"Aren't you coming too, Nanny? And I suppose I shall have to leave poor Diabolo at home too. How horrible it is going to be."

"Whoever heard of a young lady taking a Nanny with her for her come-out, Miss Miranda," scolded Nanny, but her voice showed how pleased she was at Miranda's suggestion. "I am too old to go gallivanting up to town, Miss Miranda. You know that," she scolded. "Besides, you will be taking Helmslow with you. He will see that you behave yourself."

Miranda grinned at the thought of Helmslow, the elderly stud groom at Melbury Place. He was much more than just a groom. He was, in some ways, more like a second father to her, just as he had been almost a friend rather than a servant to her father, Sir Peter. Yes, she thought, at least she would have Helmslow with her in town.

Nanny was still scolding away in her rambling voice. "Whether Helmslow will be able to look after you is more than I can say. I wager he will have his hands full. Still, if Lady Eversley finds you a husband, then he need worry no more. You'll not be coming back to Melbury Place at all, I dare say."

Miranda stared at her in blank dismay. "I don't want

a husband, Nanny dear," she said reprovingly. Then she gave her a quick kiss on the cheek and hurried from the room as fast as her limping steps would carry her. From the frowning look on her face, it was obvious that she was thinking about the stallion, Diabolo, rather than the London treats in store for her.

Shaking her head, Nanny looked after her wayward charge. "You're too much the tomboy, Miss Miranda," she said out loud to the retreating figure. "What you need is a good strong husband to make you behave like the proper young lady you should be."

2

Lady Dorothy Eversley gazed complacently down upon the magnificent staircase of her London house. Her party, she decided with more than a touch of relief, was a definite success. The London season had hardly begun, but she had nevertheless managed to fill her drawing rooms with the greater part of the glittering throng who made up polite society.

Of course, she had known that it would be all right. Not for nothing had she given a succession of successful social gatherings over the past ten years. It was perhaps true that she had not quite attained the fame of Lady Jersey as a hostess, but nevertheless she had never given a party that could be called a sad affair. In her own way, she thought, she was a notable hostess. The food and the wine were always of the best, and the company never contained anybody who might be thought the tiniest bit vulgar.

Guests were thronging up the staircase, and outside she could hear the rattle of the carriages, as they drove up to the front door and deposited yet more partygoers. As each couple trod up the red carpet, their names were boomed out: "The duke and duchess of Westhampton . . . Sir Horace Walpole . . . the Honorable Mr. James Martock."

"Dear Mr. Martock," she mumured to the latest arrival. He was a middle-aged man, soberly dressed, but with a good-humored countenance. He bent low over her hand, clasping it with perhaps just a little too much enthusiasm for mere friendliness. "So good of you to support me with your presence here tonight," said Lady Eversley smiling happily.

"You do not seem to need my support," said Mr. Martock, looking round the thronged rooms and the staircase, up which more people were proceeding.

"Perhaps not," agreed Lady Eversley, "but I am glad you are here all the same, Mr. Martock. I couldn't enjoy myself without you. I know I can rely on you to dance with all the ugliest girls, and keep the dowagers happy at the card table. So kind you are. But you must say good evening to my niece, Miss Melbury. It is *her* coming out ball, after all."

The good-humored gentleman turned to the slim girl standing a little behind her aunt. With ponderous gallantry, he took her hand and kissed it. "Miss Melbury is so beautiful she will have all the young men round her like flies after honey," he said solemnly. "But an older man like me perhaps can be forgiven for finding the aunt even more beautiful than her beautiful niece." He looked as if he might have said more, but an exquisitely dressed woman claimed Lady Eversley's attention. Mr. Martock gave way therefore to Lady Jersey.

Married to an English peer, and daughter of an Irish bishop, Lady Frances Jersey was both handsome and malicious. Small in stature, she was great in importance, for as one of the Whig hostesses she held sway over the world of high society. Woe betide the woman who incurred Lady Jersey's wrath. If she was the mother of a hopeful daughter, she would pay for it. For Lady Jersey was one of the powerful patronesses of Almack's, that center for suppers, gossip, and dancing.

Should Lady Jersey take a dislike to one of the debutantes, she could blight her career at the outset by refusing her one of the valued vouchers that gave admittance to Almack's. The Wednesday night balls were an essential part of any social season—as Lady Eversley well knew. It was with delighted enthusiasm, therefore, that she greeted her next guest.

"Dearest Frances. How good of you to come," gushed Lady Eversley. As she embraced her rival, she noted with satisfaction that Lady Jersey was wearing a purple silk gown, which made her look *positively* matronly.

"My sweet Dorothy," gushed back Lady Jersey. "What a splendid party. So this is your niece," she said, looking at Miranda's curtseying figure. "Nice girl. I must get her vouchers for Almack's. Remind me, Dorothy, if I forget."

As she swept on by, Lady Eversley heaved a sigh of relief. "Well, my dearest Miranda, that is settled," she said with pleasure. "I knew there would be no difficulty, of course. Almack's could hardly bar the niece of Lady Eversley. But it is so nice to have the vouchers offered, instead of having to ask for them."

"Is Almack's so important?" asked Miranda wonderingly.

"Important? What a country bumpkin you are, child. Without the entrance to Almack's, you might as well go back to the country. My dear, they are absolutely rigid about whom they admit. Only a few years ago they turned away the Duke of Wellington himself, because he attempted to enter wearing trousers instead of panta-loons."

"Oh," was all that Miranda could find to say. In her heart of hearts, she rather despised the fashionable world of Almack's. Imagine turning away the hero of Waterloo because he was wearing the wrong garments! How stupid it all seemed.

Lady Eversley was chattering on. "Well, my dear, the party is a great success. Everybody is here. Well, almost everybody. Lady Jersey, Beau Brassey . . . all we need now is the Earl of Templecombe. But I must not be *too* ambitious. Ten to one he will think it too early in the season for a coming-out ball."

"Do you know the Earl of Templecombe well?" asked Miranda in dismay.

"Well, of course, I have a positive *tendre* for him, as all us ladies do. He is quite a rake, in fact, but so extremely fashionable. Rakes always seem to be fashionable, don't they? If he should take a fancy to you . . . but there, I am dreaming."

"I hope he doesn't take a fancy to me, as you put it," said Miranda sternly. "I have met the Earl of Templecombe, and I didn't like him at all. In fact he nearly killed me with his curricle. He was driving so fast. We had rather an argument about it."

"Dearest Miranda, please do not tell anybody about it," said her aunt in dismay, looking round to make sure nobody had overheard. "The earl is a leader of fashion. Not that he is a Beau or a fashionable dresser, you understand. But I assure you that he can make or break you—and me, for that matter. If Templecombe says you are a bore, then very few young men will take any notice of you. If, on the other hand, he should distinguish you with his attentions, which I must say, love, doesn't seem likely from what you have told me, why then you would immediately become an established beauty. What Temple-combe says, goes with most of our young men."

"I see," said Miranda thoughtfully. "Well, I shall be-have myself, Aunt. I will not be rude to him, even if he does provoke me."

"I don't suppose he will even bother to come to-night," said her aunt gloomily. "But you must not be downcast, my dear. I see you are going to be a success, whether or not we can boast of Templecombe as a guest. Several young men have positively ogled you already, and I am of the opinion that you will stand comparison with any of the beauties here tonight."

As she spoke, Lady Eversley cast a satisfied eye over her protegée. The girl was looking beautiful and would do her credit. There could be no denying it. Of course, dark beauties were unfortunately not fashionable at the moment, now that blondes were all the rage. But Lady Eversley doubted whether even the most fastidious con-noisseur of female beauty could have resisted the com-bination of blue eyes and raven-black curls. The slightly tip-tilted nose, the oval face, and the azure eyes that sparkled with gaiety, all these added up to an undeniable and unusual charm.

Miranda was dressed perfectly, too. Lady Eversley al-most shuddered at the recollection of the tomboyish figure who had been delivered at her door, two weeks earlier. Despite the fashion plates of *La Belle Assemblée* that she had so consistently sent her niece by the weekly coaches, she had looked a perfect fright. She had been wearing a sober gray dowdy dress, and when asked, Miranda had casually said that she thought it was suitable for traveling "because it is the one I wear to go round the stables."

It had, indeed, been just the sort of reaction one

might have expected from a schoolboy, thought Lady Eversley. Nor was the rest of her niece's wardrobe much better. True, she had possessed several riding habits of exquisite cut, which Sir Peter must have ordered from London, sending his daughter's measurements. But the dresses had all been dowdy versions of the fashion plates, of a sort that simply shouted "provincial dressmaker" at the onlooker. And—Lady Eversley did shudder—there had been that shocking suit of boy's riding clothes.

The first thing to do had been to take her niece straight to a Bond Street modiste, to rig her out immediately with a complete new set of clothes. "Mademoiselle Geneviève will understand," she told her bewildered niece. "I have told her that you have lived retired in the country all this while, and of course it is the only thing that can explain your preposterous garments."

"Do I really need all these new clothes?" Miranda had asked in bewilderement, as her aunt ordered pelisses, spencers, day dresses, afternoon dresses, ball gowns, fur tippets, traveling cloaks, bonnets, Lyonese shawls, white kid half boots, Limerick gloves, reticules, muffs, ostrich feathers, and a thousand other knickknacks, including no less than a dozen pairs of silk stockings.

"You need all of them," said her aunt firmly. "I have instructed Dunn, my dresser, to throw away everything you came with except your riding habits. They, at least, will do. You need not be ashamed of them, but the rest of your clothes, my dear Miranda, are a disaster. No, do not argue with me," she added, seeing a mutinous look on her niece's face. "I know best in this. Clothes are vital, my dear. We go on very differently in the town, you know, from the country. I daresay that you do not care very much what you wore there, but here it is of first importance to be well dressed, if you wish to hold your own in society."

"I think clothes are boring," said Miranda, not altogether truthfully. "I *like* some of my old clothes. I get particularly fond of some things, Aunt Dorothy, and I *won't* have them just thrown away. Especially not the breeches."

"Miranda, you simply cannot wear such garments. They are utterly outrageous," wailed her aunt. "If anybody sees you, you will be ruined forever. It is simply not done."

Miranda realized that her aunt was truly worried. "All right, Aunt Dorothy," she said reluctantly. "I will be a good girl and not wear my breeches. But you must not throw them away, nor my stable frock. I don't mind about the other clothes, but I want to keep those. They remind me of Melbury Place." And of my father, she wanted to say. But the thought of those carefree days galloping on the turf with Sir Peter was almost too much to bear.

"Very well, child," said her aunt indulgently, and fell to discussing exactly what color shawl she should have with the muslin walking-out dress.

The huge pile of new clothes from Mademoiselle Geneviève and other Bond Street stockists were only a beginning for Miranda. Back at Lady Eversley's smart London house in Eaton Square, Miss Dunn, Lady Eversley's dresser and lady's maid, took command. There was hardly a dress, thought Miranda, that she did not alter. The addition of a flounce here, the change in a ribbon there, a small alternation in fit or the subtraction of a furbelow—all were made after a serious session of trying on. By the end of several days, Miranda ached from having to stand still while garments were tried on, prinked, pulled, and generally hung about her.

Yet she had to admit that all this effort seemed to be worthwhile when she saw the change in herself. "I hope Miss Melbury will understand if I say that she has a lovely head of hair," said Miss Dunn gravely to the by now cowed Miranda. "But I think that her curls need *working on.*"

Miranda looked gloomily at the mane of tumbling black curls that fell round her face. "Must they be cut? I like them long," she said in a depressed tone of voice.

Miss Dunn rightly took no notice of this shocking lack of enthusiasm. "À la Titus, I think," she said to Lady Eversley, and set to work clipping off the long tumbling curls. Not for Lady Eversley the attentions of a visiting hairdresser, however fashionable. Miss Dunn was the equal to any fancy Frenchman and had always done my lady's hair.

"And, Miranda, I must tell you that Dunn is extremely skillful," said Lady Eversley, looking. "You could not do better. How fortunate that your hair curls naturally. We shall not have to use curling tongs."

Miss Dunn merely smiled somewhat grimly. But Miranda had to admit that under her skillful touch, the untidy locks of hair were magically transformed. In the mirror there grew a portrait of a fashionable young stranger whose hair was parted in the middle, combed smoothly towards the sides, where curls fell over the ears and some few tiny ones in disorder upon the forehead.

Tonight, the night of the coming-out ball that was to introduce Miranda to the haut monde of fashionable life, Lady Eversley could feel nothing but pride in her protegée. Gone was the hectic tomboy who had arrived in London. In her place was a beautifully gowned young girl, exquisitely turned out, yet with a naive air about her which her ladyship privately considered the most taking thing about her.

Lady Eversley had given a great deal of thought to Miranda's first ball gown. It was important that the girl should be properly turned out, and yet her coloring was one which would look commonplace wearing the ordinary white gown suitable for a young girl. That jet-black hair, wild-rose coloring, and bluest of blue eyes was so striking that Lady Eversley decided it must be emphasized rather than concealed.

Miranda was dressed in a silk slip in French rose color, made tight to the body and very short in the waist. Over it was a white gauze frock, the bosom embroidered with rosebuds to correspond with the slip. Round the bottom were wreaths of embroidered roses. The color brought out Miranda's delicately rosy cheeks. White long gloves, a white satin reticule, and white satin shoes, also with an embroidered rosebud, completed the ensemble.

Lady Eversley had thought even longer about jewelry. At first she had plundered her own jewel box, and lent Miranda several bracelets and a tiara. "Your dear mother's jewelry is a little old-fashioned," she had said gently but truthfully. But further thought had convinced her that these aids to beauty were unnecessary in the case of her niece. With her black curls à la Titus, she had simply added headdress roses, fancifully placed to one side among the dusky locks. A simple strand of pearls round the neck drew attention to the slim shoulders that rose out of the embroidered dress.

Truly Miranda outshone most of the other girls of her year, thought Lady Eversley fondly. Perhaps her dark hair was strictly speaking unfashionable, but, beside her, Lady Eversley thought, even the most exquisite blonde looked somehow insipid. Even the lovely Diana Hatfield, until now widely acknowledged the beauty of the season, with her gold hair and green eyes, looked positively washed out when compared with jet black curls and sparkling blue eyes.

The last guests had trooped up the stairs, and Lady Eversley, her duty as hostess done as far as greeting them was concerned, was preparing to move into the crowded ballroom with her young niece. Just then a late arrival was announced. "The Earl of Templecombe."

At the top of the stairs, Lady Eversley could not help swelling slightly with pride. She clasped her hands, enjoying every second of her triumph. For even Lady Jersey must acknowledge it to be so. She gazed with pride and happiness at the tall figure of the earl coming casually up the long staircase.

He was soberly dressed compared with many of the young men who had arrived earlier. At the age of thirty-two, the Earl of Templecombe had given up the kickshaws of fashion in favor of a simpler style that knowledgeable connoisseurs of dress maintained owed something to the now disgraced Beau Brummell. Nothing about the earl's clothes, except perhaps the excellence of their cut. In advance of his contemporaries, he chose to wear black for evening wear, and in this he differed from Beau Brummell whose chosen color had been blue. Among his contemporaries who favored many colors, from blue to bottle green, the earl struck a somber note. But even those who maintained that his choice of black was a deliberately gloomy one, acknowledged that the cut of his coat and his skin-tight black knee breeches could not be faulted. He wore his clothes as if he had been poured into them by his valet.

But it was his cravats that inspired the most envy,

particularly among the younger set who had aspirations to dandyism. This evening the earl sported a cravat of amazing complexity. It was rumored that he lightly starched the muslin, to get the exact blend of stiffness and pliability. It was also rumored that he spent as much as three hours, while his valet tied cravat after cravat, to get the exact effect, it being universally known that "whatever style may have been adopted in putting on the cravat, when the knot is once formed, it should not be changed under any pretense whatever." But intimates of the earl merely laughed when this was put to them, maintaining that the earl was not one to waste time with his valet when he might be about the town doing better things with his time.

"Lady Eversley, your servant, Ma'am," said the earl, bowing gracefully over her hand.

"Lord Templecombe, I am delighted you could find time for my little ball," said Lady Eversley. "I should like to introduce you to my niece, Miranda."

"Miss Melbury, delighted. We have met before." He bowed a second time over Miranda's hand, and standing upright again said to the eager hostess beside him, "Miss Melbury and I are old friends."

Lady Eversley smiled with pure pleasure, drinking in the scene. She had not mentioned Miranda's encounter on the road, for fear that the earl might take the occasion to say he had forgotten, or to offer some other withering snub. As it turned out, all must be well.

Miranda looked rather doubtfully at the man in front of her. Talk of him and her being "old friends" brought back to mind the memory of that confusing moment when he had kissed her. Her cheeks flushed ever so slightly at the thought. But she determined not to show either embarrassment or displeasure. Had not Lady Eversley told her that the earl was a person of importance in the fashionable world?

"Yes, we are old friends," she said daringly. "Lord Templecombe rescued me, when my horse had bolted. But that seems so long ago, now that I have come to London, that I can scarcely remember what happened."

"I remember every moment exactly and in fondest detail," said the earl, smiling in what Miranda considered was a sinister way.

She knew he too was thinking of the kiss. Well, she would give as good as she got. Forgetting her promise to Lady Eversley to be polite to him at all costs, she said to him, "Good gracious, my lord. Now that you remind me, I remember that I was most upset at the time."

Lady Eversley gazed at the pair of them with some confusion. She could sense that some kind of current of feeling was running between them but could not tell whether it was excitement or hostility. "Well, I am sure my niece is most obliged to you, Lord Templecombe," she said with an air of covering up an embarrassing social silence. "We were just going into the ballroom. Will you accompany us?"

"It will be my pleasure." He bowed again with a politeness that Miranda thought was deliberately mocking. "Might I have the pleasure of this dance with Miss Melbury?"

"Thank you, my lord." She made her voice deliberately sweet, and dropped a flirtatious curtsy. If he was determined to tease her, then she would fight back by flirting.

When they entered the ballroom, he swept her into a waltz. Miranda almost gasped at the speed of it all. Fortunately she had been given lessons immediately on her arrival in London by her aunt, whose first care, after the new clothes, was to ensure that her niece would not be ill at ease on the dance floor. She had been alarmed to realize that Miranda had never learned the rudiments of dancing, preferring instead lessons in horsemanship.

The waltz, which Miranda was dancing so rapidly with the earl, had been introduced in 1807 and staider persons had maintained that it was "calculated to lead to the most licentious consequences." Waltzing sedately in her aunt's ballroom, in the firm but sexless grasp of the little French dancing master, Miranda had wondered why the waltz had been so condemned. Dancing with the earl was so very different, she no longer wondered.

At first she was embarrassed to be held in his arms, so close to his powerful body. But as her feet began to follow the music, and her body caught the rhythm of the dance, she began to relax. She felt quite uplifted. It was a marvelous experience.

"It is almost as much fun as jumping fences," she murmured, then wished she had bitten her tongue off. It had been such a naive thing to say.

"Do you hunt, Miss Melbury?" asked the earl. His saturnine face for a moment was softened by a smile at her last remark.

"Oh yes, my lord," she said with enthusiasm. Then thinking that perhaps that was the answer of a tomboy, she added: "Only sometimes. One must do something in the country, after all."

"Only sometimes." He was mocking her pretenses at sophistication now. "Only sometimes, Miss Melbury, and yet you have a horse like your Diabolo. It seems to me a crying shame to hunt *only sometimes* with a horse like that."

"Are you fond of horses, Lord Templecombe?" asked Miranda politely but firmly, anxious to avoid dangerous ground.

"Are you trying to change the conversation, Miss Melbury?" countered the earl with a teasing tone of voice. "Even if your memory is faulty, I have not forgotten our encounter. What a pleasure it was to meet you."

"It was shocking behavior on your part. I wonder you are not ashamed of it," said Miranda hotly, losing her patience. "It seems to me so odd that you should just kiss a girl you had never met before. Do you usually go round doing that kind of thing? It hardly seems the action of a gentleman."

"Anger suits you, Miss Melbury," was the reply. "And you know you spoiled your natural indignation by asking do I usually go round kissing girls. Well, my answer is that I do not usually. But then I do not usually meet girls of good birth who are making an exhibition of themselves wearing their brother's clothes."

"I don't have a brother," said Miranda, confused by his counter-attack. "I am an only child. My father had that suit made for me so that I could accompany him on his long rides without having to be bothered with skirts. You haven't ever suffered the intolerable tedium of having to wear a skirt on horseback, and having to ride side-saddle."

"I am thankful I have not," replied the earl in a bantering manner. "But I must confess to you that skirts, however tedious, become you better than breeches."

"Is that a compliment, Lord Templecombe?" asked Miranda flirtatiously.

"You may take it as such," he said unenthusiastically. "It is more in the way of a brotherly warning. Do not set everybody in London about with your pranks, Miss

Melbury. What may be acceptable in the country, will not do here."

Miranda was about to make an angry retort, but she bit back the words. She supposed she must not do anything to alienate the gentleman who was dancing with her. "It would never do to shock the leaders of fashion like yourself, Lord Templecombe," she said demurely. "I am only surprised that your lordship has bothered to dance with a hoyden like myself. Shall I manage to go on properly, now I am in the beau monde, I wonder?"

"I think you will go on very happily," said the earl in a dry tone. As he spoke the music came to an end. "You may be a hoyden, but you have danced with me and now your success will be assured."

Abruptly, he bowed. She curtseyed in return, pondering his words. But before she could make any sense of them, a crowd of young men thronged round her and started asking her for dances, so that she was busy promising this one the next waltz, and that one a country dance.

She was swept into a quadrille by a dashing officer of the guards. The quadrille, as well as the waltz, was now all the mode, thanks to the influence of her teacher Mr. Duval, whose advertisements stated that he "teaches the quadrilles in the most fashionable style of grace and elegance, as they are now danced in London, Bath, Paris, etc."

"Enjoyin' yourself, Miss Melbury?" asked the officer, very smart in his regimentals.

Miranda could only give him disjointed answers, as she went through her part in the dance. For one thing, she still had to concentrate on her steps, for even the great Mr. Duval's tuition could not make up for a lack of practice. For another, her attention was still held by the tall dark figure of the earl. From the corner of her eye she saw him walk toward the door. He paused for a moment for a few words with her aunt, who was standing at the edge of the dance floor with Mr. Martock by her side. Then he left the room.

Miranda feared that her military partner must have thought her very strange. She found it difficult to concentrate on what he was saying, though she gathered he was describing his regiment's part in the battle of Waterloo three years back, and was regretting how he had not joined up in time for it.

No sooner had the dance finished, than another young man claimed her for the cotillion, and another for one of the country dances, and so it continued till she was in some anxiety whether she could remember all their names.

Her last partner, a golden-haired youth with a lisp, told her about some exploits on the hunting field which she considered owed more to the adventures of Mr. Osbaldeston, the famous hunter, than to his own credit. But she smiled encouragingly, and said all that was proper, until he took her back to her aunt's side at her request, and went to fetch her some lemonade.

"My dearest Miranda," gushed her aunt in a whisper. "What marvelous good fortune. You are absolutely made now. You will be the toast of the season."

Miranda looked at her blankly. "It is true I seem to have had a lot of partners," she said naively.

"My dearest silly child, what are mere partners? The earl is what I am talking about, or do I mean who I am talking about. A mere half hour at the ball, and you are the only lady he honors with a dance. He could not have made it plainer. Not another young lady received even a moment of his conversation. No wonder Lady Hatfield is looking daggers at you. I always did think that she rated Diana's beauty too high. These insipid blondes, you know, cannot expect to get everything their own way."

Suddenly Miranda realized the significance of the earl's parting words—"now your success will be assured." He had been saying what her aunt had just said, that his attentions to her would ensure her social success. The arrogance of it struck her dumbfounded.

"Aunt Dorothy," she murmured urgently, "has the Earl of Templeceombe really got this power to make or break me? And if so, for heaven's sake, why? I find his manners sadly lacking in civility, and though his figure is perhaps pleasing, h s style of dressing seems almost drab compared with som ; of the beaux here."

"Oh la, la, Miranda, what shall I do with you?" laughed her aunt in high good humor. "The earl's drab style, as you call it, is really the logical extension of Beau Brummell's fasion. Poor Brummell had to flee abroad because of his debts, you know, but while he was here he was famed for his style of dressing. It was exceedingly plain but positively exquisite. Some say that Templecombe, indeed, influenced the Beau and that he, not Brummell, was the real leader of fashion." Lowering her voice she added: "I beg of you not to criticize the earl's manners to anybody but me, Miranda. And for heaven's sake do not antagonize him, dearest."

"I won't, Aunt Dorothy," said Miranda obediently. To change the conversation, she said, "I must say, dearest Aunt, that you are looking very fine tonight and not at all like an aunt, I think."

"I am glad you say so," said Lady Eversley, unconsciously preening a little. She was wearing a dress of Urlings patent lace over a slip of lilac-colored satin, with three French tucks of white satin falling one over the other at the edge of the border. A rich festoon brimming of white crepe surmounted these. A headdress in the shape of an Indian turban made it clear that she classed herself among the matrons rather than the young girls, and a drapery of the same material as the dress, only richly patterned, was twined negligently round her shoulders. Two rows of large pearls formed a necklace, with a Maltese cross of topazes. Topaz and pearl earrings completed her toilet.

"I am sure Mr. Martock agrees with me," added Miranda, looking slyly toward her aunt's companion, who though chatting to a dowager on his other side, kept his eyes firmly and dotingly on her aunt.

Just as she said this, Mr. Martock greeted a young man who came to talk to him. Turning to Lady Eversley, he said, "Sir Samuel Brassey craves an introduction to your niece, Lady Eversley. I have told him that perhaps with your help, he may have that honor. He is known as Beau Brassey, Miss Melbury," added Mr. Martock with a smile.

A man, about the same age as the earl, made an elaborate and courtly bow. He was slightly shorter than the earl, and his shoulders, though well set, were less powerfully built. Altogether, he gave the impression of a man more addicted to fashion than to sport.

Miranda gave him a steady look, as her aunt made the introductions. Beau Brassey, she noticed, was exquisitely dressed. Unlike the earl, he had not chosen black for his evening dress. Instead he wore a faultlessly cut bright green cutaway coat, with skin-tight yellow pantalettes which clung to his body and displayed handsome calves.

His cravat was more elaborate than that of the earl, cascading in several folds from his neck, and fastened with a large ruby pin. A matching large ruby ring sparkled on his finger, and he sported an elaborate fob and a jeweled quizzing glass. Yet for all these dandyfied attributes, he gave the impression, thought Miranda, of somehow being not a mere fashionable fribble. There was an undercurrent in his very looks that seemed to betray a man of power and influence.

"Most beautiful goddess, may I have the inestimable pleasure of leading you down to dinner?" The words were smoothly uttered with a practiced courtesy. Miranda was not sure whether she was being flattered or mocked.

She gave him one of her best curtseys and looked to her aunt for approval. Lady Eversley was smiling, obviously approving this glamorous new suitor. "I should like that very much," said Miranda primly, putting her hand on his arm.

"All the world is talking about you, Miss Melbury," observed the practiced complimenter by her side, as they went down to the supper table. "So much beauty, and so much charm have been widely admired. It is quite something to capture the attention of the Earl of Templecombe. Our young ladies have been grinding their teeth with envy."

The hint of mockery was still there. Miranda looked him straight in the face. His was not an unhandsome countenance—a strong straight nose, high cheekbones, and light-colored eyes. His chestnut-colored hair was carefully disarranged in a Brutus cut. Altogether Miranda found him pleasing, except perhaps for a hint of bad temper in the rather thick-lipped mouth.

Slightly confused by his compliments she replied decidedly: "The Earl of Templecombe honors me with his attentions, no doubt, but I cannot believe he wields such influence. It is absurd that one dance is enough to bring me into fashion. It cannot be right or good for one man to wield such influence."

"Bravo, Miss Melbury. I see you have ideas of your own." Sir Samuel Brassey effortlessly beckoned a footman with lobster patties, which he piled on his own plate after serving Miranda with one of them. Miranda noticed that he was positively greedy with food.

Having demolished one of the patties, Sir Samuel continued: "It is the way of the world, Miss Melbury, to set up leaders of fashion, and sometimes to pull them down again as they pulled down Beau Brummell. Brummell was once the mentor not only of the prince regent, but also of the earl; yet neither of them lifted a finger to rescue the poor man from his debts. He was forced to fly abroad, and now languishes in Calais in the greatest misery, I believe. The Earl of Templecombe, of course, has succeeded to his place in society, so perhaps it was too much to expect him to come to the aid of his erstwhile friend."

Miranda found the conversation slightly uncomfortable. "I have heard of Beau Brummell, the great dandy, of course," she said. "But surely he was always a poor man. Perhaps he should not have aspired to such heights in the first place."

"True, Miss Melbury," said the Beau. "Of course the Earl of Templecombe was much richer to start with. But he gambles for high stakes, and who knows how much of his fortune still remains? But I should not mention such boring things as money to a young lady like yourself, Miss Melbury."

"I am glad you do, Sir Samuel," said Miranda. "Most of the men I have danced with tonight seem to speak of mere trifles. I am interested in the truth of things. My father always brought me up to see facts as they really are, and to take my fences without shying."

"I admire your spirit, Miss Melbury," smiled Sir Samuel. "I shall not hesitate to tell you that one rumor has it that the magnificent Earl of Templecombe is short of ready funds. They say he is desperate for money, and the heiresses among this year's debutantes have been hoping that he may look for a rich wife. The lucky lady will have many advantages, of course. It is a magnificent family, even if the present incumbent of the title has not yet emulated the deeds of his ancestors. There is a large country estate, if it has not all been mortgaged, and a townhouse. Of course, to my mind it cannot compare with my own possessions, which have the great advantage of being unmortgaged and unwasted."

The mention of his own fortune made Miranda uncomfortably shy. Though she said that her father had brought her up to face facts, he had not dwelt very much on the subject of money. It might be mentioned, perhaps in a glancing reference to a well-bred family who were "as poor as church mice," but Sir Peter Melbury would never have dreamed of discussing his own means. He would have considered it the height of vulgarity.

"Well, I daresay that I do not give the earl his due," said Miranda in a light voice, anxious to end this discussion of money. "After all, he and I nearly had a serious accident when we last met." As the words left her lips, she regretted having mentioned the incident. She had meant to keep secret the details of that encounter in the country lane.

Sir Samuel was all ears. "You seem to be reluctant to recall the details of that encounter, Miss Melbury," he said in a silky voice that brought a flush to her cheeks. He was too perceptive, thought Miranda.

Hating herself as she did so, Miranda found herself

telling him all about it. Certain details—her masculine attire—she suppressed. And, of course, she left out altogether any mention of that shocking moment when the earl had kissed her. "I suppose I was riding too fast, but he was driving at a reckless pace," she ended. "He was abominably rude."

"I can see that you are a bruising rider. Do you ride in the park?" Sir Samuel adroitly changed the subject, seeing her embarrassment. But a half smile lingering round his slightly moist lips suggested that he knew there was more to Miranda's annoyance than she had explained.

"I should like to ride in the park, but I did not bring my own horses," said Miranda rather wistfully. "If only I had Diabolo here. He is my black stallion, whom I bred as a foal and broke myself," she explained. "But I could not bring him. He is really not the sort of horse for a polite young lady. I suppose I could borrow something from my aunt's stables, but I fear it would be a deplorable slug after Diabolo."

"That would never do, Miss Melbury. A young lady like yourself needs proper mounting," said the Beau. "You must allow me to lend you a hack."

"I don't know whether that would be possible, Sir Samuel," said Miranda doubtfully. For once she did not have to pretend she was prim. She felt a curious reluctance to accept favors from the man by her side.

Sir Samuel simply smiled a little more. "Miss Melbury," he said, "I would like to introduce you to my cousin, Miss Jennifer Brassey."

As he spoke, a rather faded woman in her thirties was passing. Sir Samuel gestured toward her and she came over to them. "Jennifer, allow me to present Miss Melbury," said Sir Samuel.

Miranda dropped a polite curtsey. Miss Brassey's appearance surprised her. Unlike Sir Samuel, she was dressed in a very understated way in a ball gown of gray satin. Though the material was rich enough, there were barely any frills or decoration, simply a touch of piping round the hem and bodice. Long gray gloves, and a rather ugly set of garnets—a necklace, a brooch, and a bracelet—completed her ensemble. Miss Brassey was a dowd. There could be no greater contrast to the dandified man by Miranda's side.

"So pleased to meet you, Miss Melbury." The faded eyes flickered. Miranda was reminded—she could not think why—of some kind of reptile. The slightest hint of malice seemed to lie in those flickering eyes. Miss Brassey smiled as she spoke, but her smile had no warmth in it.

"Jennifer," said Sir Samuel in a tone that brooked no denial, "I was telling Miss Melbury that we could lend her a hack to ride in the park tomorrow. I had the new mare in mind. You know that she is too high-spirited for you. You were saying only the other day that you did not feel at ease on her back."

"That is true, Samuel," said Miss Brassey submissively. "I should like it above all things if Miss Melbury would be so kind as to ride her for me. I fear I am not a very daring horsewoman." Though her words were polite, even ingratiating, they held an unmistakable note of disapproval.

"Thank you, Miss Brassey," said Miranda, equally politely. "But I am sure I do not wish to inconvenience you in any way. I am not certain whether my aunt would think it correct of me to accept your kind offer."

There was another flicker of those faded eyes. Then

Miss Brassey said in a dry tone, "I am sure Lady Eversley will agree, if my cousin asks her. Why, here she is passing now."

"Lady Eversley," said Sir Samuel, taking his cousin's hint, "tell this foolish child that it is quite in order for my cousin to lend her one of her hacks."

Lady Eversley, passing in the busy and slightly preoccupied manner of the successful hostess, turned the better to see who was making this offer. "Why, Miss Brassey," she said with a note of what Miranda could recognize as insincerity, "how very kind of you to be so obliging to my niece."

"Sir Samuel has pointed out that I cannot handle the hack. I am by no means a dashing horsewoman, I fear," said Miss Brassey with a kind of faded self-deprecation. "I gather there is nothing suitable in *your* stables."

Sir Samuel broke in on the conversation, as if he could see that the discussion of hoseflesh between the two ladies was going to end in hostility. "I have been talking horses with Miss Melbury, and am anxious that she should oblige my cousin by exercising her mare," he laughed. "But I believe the chit thinks that it is improper to ride in the park with me and my cousin. Lend your approval to my pleas, Lady Eversley! I assure you that Miss Melbury will be doing me a favor."

"Well, since you put it so forcefully . . ." said Lady Eversley, still sounding slightly doubtful. "Perhaps you could call on us, Sir Samuel, and we can discuss it better. And you, too, Miss Brassey," she added as an afterthought.

"Too kind," murmured Miss Brassey in acidulated tones.

"I shall be delighted to accept your invitation to

call," said Sir Samuel, with a charm and enthusiasm that concealed his cousin's lack of fervor.

Taking Miranda's hand, he lifted it gently to his lips. The gesture was one of elaborate politeness, but as he bowed over her hand, his eyes looked at her in an unexpectedly intimate way. Miranda had the oddest sensation of panic that perhaps he was seeing her without any clothes on. She had to fight back an impulse to wrench her fingers away.

"I have a fancy to see you in the saddle, Miss Melbury," he said. "Such a spirited creature as you will look most beautiful on the mare. Au revoir. I shall live for the moment when next I see you."

While he took his leave of Lady Eversley, Miss Brassey gave her hand to Miranda. Her fingers were cold and lifeless, and lay in Miranda's palm as if they were some kind of dead animal. "I shall look forward to knowing more of you, Miss Melbury," she murmured. "My cousin is much *épris* with your charms."

The same coldly polite hand and the same few formal words were then offered to Lady Eversley, who dealt with them in a way which showed Miranda that she was covering up her distaste.

As the two Brasseys turned away, Lady Eversley smiled at her niece. "Another conquest, dear Miranda. The Beau is truly taken with you. I can tell. Well, he is as rich as Croesus, even if nobody is quite sure about his family tree. His manners, it is agreed, are universally pleasing, and he is definitely one of the smarts. Why, he is almost as fashionable as the earl, and much more courteous to the ladies."

"Do you like the Brasseys?" asked Miranda curiously.

"I adore Sir Samuel. Such charm could hardly fail to please," said her aunt. "I daresay Miss Brassey is a very good woman though I must confess, Miranda, that we are *not* bosom friends."

Miranda would have liked to ask more, but she did not wish to interrupt her aunt's duties as a hostess. "Well, dearest Aunt Dorothy," she said, "I am enjoying my come-out enormously. But I don't know what to make of what you call my conquests. Sometimes I wish I was back on Diabolo with a good run ahead and some fine fences. I am sure they would be easier to negotiate than all the obstacles of the fashionable world."

Her aunt gave a trill of laughter and a gesture of mock dismay. "Really, Miranda," she rebuked. But her eyes sparkled with pleasure. The girl was unusual, and that frank way of speaking might have been put down as a terrible fault. Fortunately, it seemed to have caught on. From now on, thought Lady Eversley, when Miranda says something outrageous, it will be put down as witty and unusual. It is the way of the world either to condemn, or to admire, eccentricity.

3

Miranda Melbury was in good spirits and the best of health. Indeed, had she been at Melbury Place on her morning tour of inspection at the stables, she would have whistled a merry tune. For, unlike most heiresses, she could whistle as tunefully as any of the grooms, and indeed was wont to join them in harmony as they whistled at their work.

Whistling, she thought wistfully, was yet another of those tomboy habits she would have to suppress, at least while she was staying with Lady Eversley. Dear Aunt Dorothy would consider it more suitable to an errand boy than a well-brought-up young lady.

In another respect she also fell short of this mythical young lady she was meant to be. After such a night of dissipation, it would have been suitable if she had stayed in bed in the morning, taking tea and toast, or bread and butter with chocolate. And a becoming paleness of the cheek might have been expected on rising.

Instead Miranda had been up for hours. She had eaten a hearty breakfast, including several slices of ham, under the approving eye of Lady Eversley's smart town butler. She had inspected the books in the library, and she had even penetrated down to the kitchens and chatted with the French chef who reigned there in dictatorial splendor. Despite this early morning activity, she showed no signs of tiredness. Her complexion was as rosy as the night before. Her step was jaunty. It might be vulgar to admit it, but Miranda was in the very tip-top of health and strength.

As she stepped into the morning room, with the vague idea of wasting a few minutes consulting the fashion plates, she was surprised to see her aunt there. Lady Eversley had spent half the morning in bed recruiting her strength after the night's ordeal, and Miranda had had little expectation of seeing her up and about much before midday. But her aunt had obviously dragged herself from her bed. She was wearing a very frivolous form of undress, a kind of peignoir which amounted to a mass of frothy lace and frills. She was poised on one of the delicate gilt chairs that adorned the morning room, and seemed to be studying a piece of paper. As she looked up at her niece's entrance, her eyes were full of tears, and her cheeks were streaked in such a way as to make clear that she had been crying.

Forgetting that politeness demanded she ignore such signs of emotion, Miranda ran over to her aunt and embraced her. "Dearest Aunt Dorothy, what on earth is the matter?"

"O Miranda, how kind of you . . . so kind . . . but I must not trouble you . . . burden you with my problems. They will be solved somehow, I am sure, though I can't for the life of me see how." Her aunt dabbed at her eyes with a very pretty but inadequate silk hankerchief.

"Is it money, dear Aunt? Is that some bill?" asked Miranda. "Please tell me. I am sure I can help."

"Nobody can help me with these," was her aunt's

melodramatic response, and in a distracted way Lady Eversley fell to crying. Miranda could not help noticing how elegantly she cried. The tears simply trickled out of her eyes, unaccompanied by the sniffs and snuffles of less elegant mortals.

"Please, Aunt Dorothy. A trouble shared is a trouble halved," coaxed Miranda, falling into one of Nanny's sayings.

"Blackmail," murmured her aunt, through the now sodden hankerchief.

"Blackmail?" Miranda could hardly believe her ears. "Why on earth should anybody want to blackmail you, dearest Aunt? Now you must tell me all about it. I may not be able to help immediately, but I shall think of something. Papa used to say that I had a very good head for business."

But Lady Eversley said nothing more. Her emotions overwhelmed her and she wept without ceasing into the hankerchief, too upset for words.

Seeing her aunt was overcome, Miranda rang for the servants. "A glass of cordial and smelling salts," she ordered, when the butler arrived.

"Should I send in Miss Dunn?" he asked with some perplexity.

"No, Stratton. Just the salts and a cordial. My aunt is a little overtired from last night's ball. I shall stay with her here." So saying, she guided the sobbing Lady Eversley from her unstable chair to a sofa at the end of the room. "Would you like Miss Dunn," she said doubtfully when the butler had disappeared. "I told Stratton not to call her. I think we should be private."

"No, no, child. The servants must not suspect . . . I will pull myself together. After all, if I am going to be ruined tears will not help me," was Lady Eversley's inconsequential reply. She paused as Stratton came in with a silver salver on which reposed the smelling salts and a glass of sinister-looking green cordial.

"Thank you, Stratton," she said firmly. The butler, with an air of reluctance, left the room. Lady Eversley sipped cautiously at the cordial, shuddering at every mouthful. She took a brief sniff at the smelling salts and seemed to make up her mind. From out of her reticule, where she had stuffed it on Miranda's entrance, she handed over a piece of paper.

With eager curiosity, Miranda took it from her. Opening out its folds, she saw that it was written in a clear but featureless hand—as if the writer had been at pains to suppress all the individuality of his handwriting. As she read it, the cause of her aunt's distress became clear.

> The writer of this letter begs to present his compliments to Lady Eversley and to inform her that some interesting correspondence between her and Mr. Philip Ambrose has come into his possession. These letters the writer is anxious to restore to Lady Eversley, for remuneration which will cover the expense of keeping them out of the hands of less genteel associates.
>
> These associates have formed the opinion that the correspondence might be of interest to Mr. James Martock. At present, the writer of this letter feels sure that Lady Eversley would prefer their return to her, without the aforementioned gentleman being brought into the matter. . . .

For a moment Miranda failed to understand the drift of the tortuous prose. Then slowly enlightenment began to dawn. "Dear Aunt Dorothy," she said impulsively, "am I right in thinking that it is more than a friendship between you and that nice man, Mr. Martock? Do you have an understanding with him?"

Lady Eversley, fidgeting self-consciously with the handkerchief, said, "Mr. Martock has been extremely attentive, my dear. Such a nice quiet man. I expect it seems very odd to you, at my advanced years, but I must confess that I have never liked being a widow. So lowering. There is something so depressing about not having a gentleman in the household . . ."

"And Mr. Martock has asked you to be his wife?" asked Miranda bluntly. Hoping to give her aunt's thoughts a slightly more optimistic turn, she added: "If so, I must congratulate him. I think you will suit admirably and be very happy."

Lady Eversley brightened at this evidence of her niece's approval. "Well, he has not asked me in so many words, my dear," she confided, "but I hope I am not such a goose as not to know when a gentleman is about to make an offer. Oh but, Miranda, what shall I do about these letters? James is such a *kind* man and so *understanding;* but he has such high principles and he thinks the world of me. The shock might make him wonder if I was fit to be his wife."

"Aunt Dorothy," said Miranda cautiously, "what exactly was in those letters? And who is Mr. Philip Ambrose? I have never heard of him."

"Poor dear Mr. Ambrose. He was such a sweet boy, and such a wonderful poet. Of course he hadn't had his verses published yet. He took such a fancy to me, Miranda. Of course it was all ridiculous. He was a good ten years younger than me, but he wrote me such delicious poems. He used to send me sonnets. I knew it was absurd, of course, but it was so reassuring at my age to have a poet sighing at my feet. Lady Jersey was mad with jealousy, I assure you. Only I fear I may have been a tiny bit indiscreet."

"You wrote to him?"

"Well, yes, I did. It seemed the least I could do, to write him a note, when he was going to all that trouble making up so many verses every week. Of course, there was no harm in the letters. Why, I distinctly remember telling him in one of them that I was far too old for him . . . But I fear that Mr. Martock might not appreciate the tone of them."

"I must say that I consider this Mr. Ambrose has behaved extremely badly," said Miranda in a disapproving voice. "I daresay that writing you verses was well within the line, but to be so careless as to let the letters you sent in reply fall into the hands of a blackmailer . . . It shows a very casual spirit, I am afraid."

Lady Eversley sat bolt upright on the sofa in a sudden fit of emotion. "You don't understand, Miranda. Poor dear Mr. Ambrose *treasured* those letters. He kept them in his waistcoat pocket, and I can well remember how he used to take them out and kiss them and say they were his dearest possessions. Why, he told me he slept with them under his pillow at night."

Miranda could not help thinking that her aunt's poetic lover must have been a very tiresome young man. But wisely she refrained from making any comment, knowing that any criticism would only outrage her aunt. She contented herself in saying, "Well, Aunt Dorothy, the fact remains that he was careless enough to lose them eventually. Unless he, himself, is the blackmailer."

Her aunt gave a shudder at the word. She snatched up the handkerchief and dabbed her eyes. "Poor Mr.

Ambrose is dead. It was almost a year ago now. He was killed in some kind of horrid street brawl in a very vulgar bit of London, where I have never been. I don't know what he can have been doing there, but I can only suppose his body was robbed and the letters found. . . ."

Miranda looked grave. This was serious. If the letters had fallen into the hands of one of the numerous criminal gangs that roamed London, then her aunt's position was indeed serious. She had no reliance on the suggestion that the letters were harmless. Aunt Dorothy was a dear, but a more indiscreet person Miranda had yet to meet. No doubt the letters *were* harmless in spirit—but they sounded as if they could be misinterpreted, to say the least. And what would Mr. Martock make of them?

"Aunt Dorothy," she said urgently, "don't you think the best and wisest thing to do would be to tell Mr. Martock everything? Let him get back the letters for you. If he truly loves you—and I am sure he does—he will understand. If you explain how it happened, he *must* do." Even as she said them, the words sounded unconvincing to her.

Lady Eversley lay back on the sofa with a smothered wail. "Miranda, I *can't*. Even if Mr. Martock understood, and I am not at all sure that he would, he will give me a terrible scold, and I hate being scolded. And perhaps he will tell his sister, Lady Roehampton, and that I couldn't bear. She is the stuffiest woman, who does nothing but good works, and is not at all like dearest James."

Miranda privately thought that in a way Mr. Martock was rather a stuffy person, but it was none of her business to say so. If her aunt was determined to keep the letters out of his hands, then there was no help for it. It was pointless to argue. She must apply her mind to the problem of getting the letters back for her aunt. "Leave it to me, dear Aunt Dorothy," she said firmly. "I will try and think out a way of dealing with this whole problem."

"But how?" cried her aunt.

Miranda had no very good notion how. But she opened the piece of paper again, which she had temporarily put aside, and read on to the end of the letter.

If Lady Eversley is prepared to bargain for her letters, she must come to the far end of Rotten Row in Hyde Park at midnight tonight, where she will find a gentleman anxious to meet her and talk terms. If she does not arrive, the letters may have to be passed to Mr. Martock.

At the bottom of the page was a mysterious postscript, which read: *Dearest golden boy, your poems make me so madly happy.*

Miranda read the postcript aloud. "What's this," she said. "It doesn't make sense. Why should the blackmailer suddenly address you as a boy?"

"It makes sense to me," said her aunt gloomily, knotting the long-suffering handkerchief. "It is something I wrote in one of the letters, I am afraid. It shows without a doubt that the villain has got them."

"I wonder who on earth the blackmailer is," said Miranda thoughtfully. "Can you think of anybody who would want to hurt you, Aunt Dorothy? The writing of the letter is in an educated hand."

"I don't think I have an enemy in the world," sobbed Lady Eversley. "Well, at least I can't think of any *gentleman . . .*"

"You don't think it could be a woman?" The sudden thought struck Miranda. "After all, though the writing doesn't look very feminine, it *might* be. What about women enemies, Aunt Dorothy?"

"Well," Lady Eversley sat up and began to cudgel her brains. "There's no denying, Miranda, that my successes *have* caused jealousy. I mean there's Lady Hatfield who must be dying to scratch my eyes out, now that you have cast her precious Diana in the shade. And, of course, Lady Jersey is a dear, dear friend, but we have had words in the past. . . . I remember telling her that I didn't think her friendship with the prince regent was at all the thing."

"Surely Lady Jersey wouldn't stoop to blackmail, dear Aunt. And Lady Hatfield may be angry about me, but surely she wouldn't go *that* far."

"I suppose not." Lady Eversley looked disgruntled, as if slightly put out that she could not solve the blackmailer's identity. There was a pause as she wracked her brain. "There was the wife of Sir John Lade—a fearfully vulgar woman, Miranda. I didn't exactly cut her but it is true that I wouldn't ask her to any of my evening parties. No, but surely . . . There's one other person. But surely it couldn't be? Or might she?"

"Who's that?" asked Miranda eagerly.

"You may not have remarked on it, dearest child," said her aunt with sudden caution, "but Miss Brassey and I do not see eye to eye. Sir Samuel is the most charming person, but I have always thought his cousin was a dowd. I believe she is friendly with Mr. Martock's sister, Lady Roehampton. Something to do with charities for fallen women or some such stuff."

"She certainly didn't seem very friendly last night," said Miranda. "But do you think she would go so far as to blackmail you, Aunt Dorothy?"

Her aunt sighed in exasperation. "No, Miranda. I don't really think that she would. She may have had her eye on Mr. Martock. All the world knows she harbored hopes in that direction well before *I* met him. But even she cannot seriously have thought that James would fall in love with a spinster who has no dress sense and next to nothing in the way of conversation."

"Never mind, Aunt Dorothy," said Miranda soothingly. It did not seem likely to her, either, that the faded Miss Brassey would stoop to such villainy. "We will foil this ruffianly blackmailer somehow. I shall keep the appointment for you in Hyde Park tonight. That way, we shall perhaps discover the identity of the blackmailer."

"Oh, Miranda, you can't go. It just isn't safe. Why, Rotton Row is a notorious place for assignations of the most vulgar kind. It is quite likely you will be put to annoyance, if not worse."

"I shall take Helmslow, my groom from home, with me, dear Aunt. He can take a pistol with him. He is absolutely devoted to me, and will make sure I come to no harm. He is totally discreet, too. And if I go in your stead, then you will not absolutely be compromised by these rogues."

"I don't think you ought to, Miranda," groaned her aunt in indecision. "If only your dear father was alive. I feel so guilty letting you go, and yet I don't know what else to do. I would go myself but ten to one I should faint, or do something silly. I do not think my nerves would stand it . . . and besides, it is tantamount to a confession that those letters *were* written by me."

"No, Aunt Dorothy, I shall go. I need not be frightened with Helmslow by my side. And if I can only set eyes on this ruffian, then I can come home, and between us we can plan what to do. I think he will probably want money."

"What shall we do if he asked an enormous sum," said Lady Eversley. "It is bound to be a big sum, I should think, for I cannot believe he would blackmail me for paltry amounts. And then what shall I do? My jointure is comfortable, of course, but I am always in debt and that horrid dressmaker duns me all the time, and bills come in every post. I shall go distracted if I have to borrow money. I have never been able to understand percentages and interest, and even those that do always seem to be absolutely rooked by them."

"Are you so poor, Lady Eversley?" asked Miranda in dismay. "I am afraid last night's ball was fearfully costly, but I did not think about it at all. Perhaps we could persuade Mr. Scrimgeour to pay for it, out of my trust funds."

"No, my dear, I am not exactly poor: I am in debt. Everybody I know is in debt," said her aunt, with remarkable sangfroid. "I have always owed money, but I am not exactly short of it, either, if you understand me. Lord Eversley looked after that kind of thing for me when we were married, of course, and it is since his death I have found it difficult not to run up debts. But if I marry Mr. Martock, I shall have no more worries. He has a good-sized estate, and he will know how to cope with all those horrid bills. Somehow I can't get in the way of paying them in time even when I do have the money."

Miranda had an impulse to laugh. She was beginning to see that her aunt, though a kindly and amusing woman, was a natural muddler with a rather shallow mind. Dear Aunt Dorothy, she thought, she really *needs* a husband to look after her. If only she felt we could tell Mr. Martock. . . .

Or the Earl of Templecombe. The thought popped unbidden into her mind. If she could tell the earl, he would surely help her. She could not believe that the strong powerful man could not deal with a set of paltry blackmailers.

She shook herself. It was an absurd notion. After all, the earl was nothing more than a man she had met twice, and on one of those occasions (Miranda blushed to herself) he had behaved more like a rake than a gentleman. How could a loose-living man like him be of help to her?

As she pondered in her mind how best to deal with the problem, she was amazed at Lady Eversley's spirits. One moment her aunt had been talking in despair, the next she was chatting happily about the latest fashions. For once Miranda had promised to keep the mysterious assignation with the blackmailer in her aunt's place, it was as if Lady Eversley immediately threw off her cares and put the whole horrid business quite out of her mind.

Miranda would have been angry at this apparent unconcern but for the fact she realized her aunt could not help it. Lady Eversley was a good-natured woman, but not a deep thinker. Her mind was shallow and unable to think of more than one thing at a time. If something unpleasant occurred she was cast down, then after exclaiming at it and complaining, she would put the whole thing out of her mind just like that.

Miranda only wished she could do so too. She spent an uneasy day with her aunt, visiting even more fashionable dressmakers in the Bond Street area. Lady Jersey's ball was the next glittering occasion that took place. All the polite world would be there, and it was important, said Lady Eversley, that Miranda should be as exquisitely gowned as ever.

"Nothing is more sinking to the spirits than to know that one's clothes are not quite up to the mark," she said seriously to her niece, as they inspected yet another bale of material, this time of *gros de Chine.*

"You need a carriage pelisse and bonnet, too, Miranda," she said suddenly. "You cannot go gallivanting round Hyde Park without it. I suggest this Cachemire material. You see, it has a very pretty bonnet of matching vermillion satin, and straw-colored ribbands," she said, pointing to a very elegant pelisse of white with a vermillion-colored belt.

"Oh, Aunt Dorothy, there isn't time for a new pelisse," said Miranda wearily. "Besides I know what I must wear." She felt quite out of charity with her aunt, whose mind now seemed to run easily on clothes for an occasion that Miranda dreaded.

At last yeilding to her aunt's suggestion, she brought a pair of white kid half boots, and some Limerick gloves to go with her own pelisse. After all, thought Miranda, they will come in useful anyway.

Somehow the day dragged along with shopping, a light luncheon, afternoon calls, and all the frippery conversation which might be expected of the fashionable world. Miranda thought it would never come to midnight.

She had told Helmslow that he must accompany her, and asked him to bring a pistol with him. The gray-haired groom who had helped her onto her first pony, taken her hunting for the first time, and spent many hours with the little girl who insisted on hanging round the stables, just nodded grimly at her odd request. With the freedom of an old family retainer he said, "Miss Miranda, you are up to your tricks again."

"Oh, but Helmslow, I am not, really I am not. I can't tell you about it because it is not my secret, but I am relying on you to be with me so that nothing awful happens. Only I really can't explain. What I do know is that, if Papa were alive, he would approve of what I am doing."

The old servant looked skeptical at this, and muttered something which Miranda could not quite catch. But after a pause he merely said, "Do you expect trouble, Miss Miranda? Likely I should take one of the stable lads with me."

"No, no," said Miranda impatiently. "We will take the carriage to the park. Then you and I will go to the end of Rotten Row. I have to meet . . . somebody there, Helmslow, and I think it would be safer if you could be within eyesight, though without him seeing you. I can't be seen to have you with me, but if you could just be a little behind me, so that you are near enough to come to my aid if I should call out for help . . ."

"Don't you worry, Miss Miranda. I shall see to it you come to no harm, though I wonder myself what you are doing," he said gruffly. Miranda felt she could not explain further, but she was comforted to think that he would be with her. It was beginning to be clear to her that she had undertaken a very dangerous engagement. There might be all kinds of frisky young gentlemen and rakes abroad for their assignations at this hour. And a tough ruffian, of course, might turn up at the rendezvous. It was a very frightened girl who set out from the house at Eaton Square at half past eleven that evening.

Lady Eversley, who had cried off the evening entertainment they had originally meant to attend with the excuse of a headache, saw her off at the door. "Dearest Miranda, I am so grateful to you . . . do not take any risks. I know Helmslow will look after you."

Miranda did not entirely share her confidence as, clutching a camel-hair scarf around her, she set out.

Though the elderly groom climbed in beside her, Miranda was not entirely sure whether his protection would be adequate. Poor Helmslow would be no match for a gang of ruffians. Then she recollected that the annoymous letter had been written in an educated hand, and felt slightly less nervous.

Far from wearing the elaborate white and vermillion pelisse that her aunt had tried to buy for her that afternoon, Miranda was dressed very plainly. She had put on the dull gray dress in which she had arrived at Eaton Square. Lady Eversley had demanded that it should immediately be given to one of the kitchen maids, "for even Betty the housemaid would think it unfashionable, dearest, and Dunn would never dream of wearing such a sad thing," but Miranda had insisted on keeping it, and was glad that she had done so. She decided that it would be best if she looked as discreet, not to say mousy, as possible, in the hope that no casual passerby would recognize her. Not that there would be many passersby from the haunt ton at this time of night, she hoped.

After all, fashionable London would either be at the last act of the opera, or at Lady Hatfield's soirée, or, in the case of the gentlemen, gambling for high stakes at one of the clubs or the low gaming dens round Mayfair's Clifford Street. And even if they were about more nefarious pursuits with members of her own sex, thought Miranda, they would surely be in the luxurious houses she had heard of, rather than keeping midnight rendez-vous. . . . She resolutely turned her mind away from a thought which was unladylike in the extreme.

As the carriage stopped at the nearest point of the road round the park, Miranda took a deep breath. This was it. "Are you prepared, Helmslow?" she whispered, even though she knew that nobody could have heard her inside the carriage. "After I go, you follow me at a discreet distance so that nobody can tell that we are together. Do not interfere, I beg of you, unless I call for your assistance. Do you understand, Helmslow? *No matter what happens,* wait for my call for you. Else, you will ruin all."

The old groom only grunted, and with that Miranda had to be content. She was glad he would be near at hand, for her heart was beating with fear. As she got down from the carriage, it almost was too much for her. Her courage failed, and it was only with the greatest of effort that she was able to walk toward the end of Rotten Row.

The park was darker by night than she had expected. Although it was full moon, she had not realized that the trees would cast such black shadows across the grass. In the distance moonbeams picked out the wooly backs of the sheep that grazed the grass to a manageable level, and shafts of silver light danced among the tree trunks. To the eye of a poet it would have been an idyllic scene. No doubt the late Mr. Ambrose would have produced some very pretty verse, thought Miranda savagely. But for a young girl, faced with an assignation with a ruthless blackmailer, the moonlight was more sinister than picturesque.

She walked toward the end of the Row with a deliberately brisk gait. In the side of her vision, she had noticed figures in one of the shrubs. Her heart almost stopped beating for a second, until their movements showed unmistakably that they were a pair of open-air lovers, rather than footpads. It was shocking, no doubt, that such things should go on, but Miranda could not help being relieved that they were more concerned with each other than herself.

The end of the Row was completely deserted. She looked round cautiously but could see nobody. Was it too early? She stood still and strained her ears to listen for the slightest sound. From the far part of the park she could hear the faint baaing of the sheep, and from the bushes she had passed, the rustle of lovers' whispered conversation.

A cloud passed over the moon and the crisscross patterns of the moonlight and its shadows were dimmed into darkness. Miranda could hear footsteps behind her. She whirled round to face whoever it might be.

A tall figure was coming straight toward her. As he approached, the moon reappeared from behind the cloud, casting its striking pale light upon the face of . . . Miranda gasped . . . the Earl of Templecombe.

He halted. His face registered amazement, an emotion that was mirrored on Miranda's own countenance. Then with his inimitable casual grace, he made his bow. "Delighted to meet you so unexpectedly, Miss Melbury," he drawled. "Do you ramble by moonlight, or am I intruding upon a lover's rendez-vous?"

Miranda was speechless. For a moment it seemed as if the whole world stood still. Somewhere inside her was a welter of emotions in which surprise, shock, anger, dismay, and some other feeling that she could not identify, raged for mastery. Pressing her hands together, she managed a formal curtsey in reply. It steadied her nerves. "I suppose you could say that I am here to make a rendez-vous, Lord Templecombe," she managed. "I must suppose that you are the unknown gentleman I have come to meet . . ."

"I am honored, if surprised that you should cast me in such a role," said the earl coming close to her. "I must confess, for my own part, that I was not expecting you,

69

Miss Melbury. It was quite a different lady with whom I had an assignation tonight."

Before she could say anything, with a deft move he put his arm round her waist and pulled her toward him. As he did so, he tilted up her chin with his other hand, so that her face was raised to him.

With a violent jerk, Miranda pulled away. Choking with fury, she hissed at him, "How dare you touch me! I despise you. You are worse than a rake . . . you are a disgrace to the name of gentleman."

The man who was holding her was as strong as iron. She found herself struggling within a relentless grip. He held her against her will, and for a second she thought that for the second time he was going to steal a kiss. Then suddenly it was all over. He let her go. He pushed her away from him.

Miranda swayed, as if she might fall to the ground. But suddenly realizing that a third person had arrived on the scene, she pulled herself upright with a heroic effort of will. It was Sir Samuel Brassey. "Sir Samuel," she gasped. "I seem to have lost my way in the park. I know you will help me."

He stood in front of the earl so that Miranda was slightly behind him. This time, instead of his usually dandified clothing, he was wearing just a velvet midnight-blue cloak, but his hand was meaningfully by his side, on what seemed to be the hilt of a sword. "Is this gentleman annoying you, Miss Melbury?" he said, affecting not to recognize the earl.

It was an appalling dilemma for Miranda. She could not begin to explain anything to the Beau. In what she hoped seemed a controlled way, she tried a laugh. "Not exactly, Sir Samuel. It is my fault. I seem to have lost my way. I had a sudden whim to see Hyde Park by moonlight. My groom is somewhere near me, but he seems to have wandered away. Helmslow?" she raised her voice for him. "Oh, thank goodness, there you are."

Out of the shadows stepped the reassuringly solid figure of Helmslow. She could see the bulge where he carrid his pistol in the pocket of his greatcoat. His appearance lowered the emotional temperature. It was now impossible for the two men to quarrel, with a servant standing by. "Oh, Helmslow," she said hurriedly, "I am glad you have arrived. Lord Templecombe and Sir Samuel Brassey are both here tonight, like myself, to see the moonlight. Is it not odd? I know you two gentleman will think me extremely eccentric, but I vow I am ravished by the prettiness of the scene. But I must go."

"I will accompany you to your carriage, Miss Melbury . . . to make sure that no passerby molests you. The place is full of Cits," said Sir Samuel firmly. "It was perhaps a little unwise for you to come here in search of the moonlight. It is a spot well known for, let us say, amorous encounters of a kind that can mean nothing to a well-brought-up young lady like yourself." The words, it seemed to Miranda, were addressed to the earl.

Obviously Sir Samuel thought that the earl had come this way in search of a woman—possibly he thought she had been inveigled into this improper assignation. She could say nothing to dull his suspicions. The truth—that she had come to meet a blackmailer who had turned out to be the earl—was infinitely more shocking.

"Thank you, Sir Samuel." She did not have the spirit to say more. After all, she had, in the agony of the moment, more or less appealed for his help. Her savior offered his arm to her, with a smile she did not much care for. Very formally the two men bowed to each other.

Sir Samuel led her away from the earl. His tall figure stayed there, lounging in the moonlight.

After they had gone a little on the way back to the carriage, with Helmslow keeping a discreet distance behind just out of earshot, Sir Samuel said, "Miss Melbury, would you take the advice of an admirer?"

"Yes of course, Sir Samuel. But I assure you that it was not how you must be thinking it was. Oh . . . I cannot explain."

"Explanations are not necessary, Miss Melbury," replied the Beau, in a silky voice. "To me you are perfect. Nothing you do can be wrong. Spirited behavior simply adds to your charms. You are never insipid, Miss Melbury. But I feel I must nonetheless warn you the moonlight walks are something a little more than unconventional. You may trust me, Miss Melbury, not to tell a soul about it. But it would, I fear, injure your reputation should such stories get around."

Miranda felt very uncomfortable indeed. She did not like the tone of his compliments, especially said to her in such a lonely place. Thank goodness Helmslow was within call. At the same time there was nothing he had said to which she could raise an objection. She felt powerless. His remarks about her conduct injuring her reputation particularly lowered her. It was almost as if he was threatening her.

She forced herself to murmur, "You are so kind, Sir Samuel." To her relief the Beau did not say more. As Miranda entered the carriage, he took her hand. He raised it to his lips as if to kiss it in the formal manner. Then turning it round, so that it was palm upward, he pressed his hot lips into the center. They lingered there, it seemed, for an age.

"Thank you, Sir Samuel," blurted out Miranda, as

she pulled her hand away in an agony of embarrassment. As Helmslow climbed in after her, she was again full of gratitude for his fatherly presence. She would have taken her handkerchief to wipe away the lingering feeling of Sir Samuel's kiss, except that it would draw the groom's attention.

Helmslow sat very upright during the whole journey and did not say a word. It was obvious that he was awaiting an explanation. Miranda simply could not offer one. The aura of his disapproval in the carriage was overwhelming but there was nothing much, she thought, that she could do about it.

For her own part, she felt, above everything, tired. An exhaustion so total as to drive out almost every other feeling, overwhelmed her. She arrived at the Eaton Square house too fatigued to think straight.

Wearily she thought she must now explain everything to her aunt, but to her surprise, and dismay, Lady Eversley was already asleep. Miranda had imagined her restlessly awaiting her arrival, all on edge to discover her fate. Instead Lady Dorothy Eversley had simply taken herself to bed, and even now was enjoying a harmless slumber free from worries. "She meant to stay up, Miss Melbury," said Stratton, who had waited up for her. "But my lady could not keep her eyes open. Would you like a glass of hot milk, she ordered me to ask you?"

"No, thank you, Stratton," said Miranda, a sense of anticlimax creeping over her. "I shall go to bed too."

4

The next morning Miranda had yet another insight into the butterfly mind of her aunt. Her ladyship was following her usual custom of having bread and butter and a cup of chocolate in the privacy of her bedchamber, rather than attend the breakfast table downstairs where more substantial viands were on offer.

Miranda had already refreshed herself from the substantial array of eggs, slices of bacon, grilled kidneys, cold ham, and cold beef, which was laid out on the sideboard of the breakfast room. The ubiquitous Stratton had attended her, pressing her to a little more beef and persuading her that not to try the kidneys would be to insult the staff in the kitchen.

Satisfied with an enormous meal, Miranda decided that she could not wait until her aunt had dressed. Instead she would attend her in her bedchamber. It was there that she discovered her, disdainfully munching a paper-thin slice of bread and butter.

"Would you not like some of the cold ham?" she asked her aunt. "I could order Stratton to bring some up from the breakfast table. There are grilled kidneys too. They are awfully good."

"Ham. How horrid. No, my dear child, Stratton knows that I cannot face cold meats at this unreasonable hour in the morning. I am perfectly satisfied with bread and butter." Lady Eversley relaxed, sighing into her pillows, which her dresser Dunn obligingly had plumped up for her.

Miranda looked doubtfully at Miss Dunn, who was hovering round the dressing table placing little pots here and rearranging hairpins there. She would have preferred to talk without the dresser's somewhat depressing presence.

"My dearest Miranda, do you know what?" said Lady Eversley in the hushed tones of one about to convey a bombshell of alarming information.

"No, dear Aunt?" Miranda was immediately all attention. What on earth was her aunt going to tell her? It must be something frightful to take Lady Eversley's mind off the otherwise all-important matter of last night's encounter with the blackmailer.

"The prince regent is giving a musical soirée next month, and he has specifically asked for you and me to dine beforehand at Carleton House," said her aunt triumphantly.

"Well?" was all Miranda said. She was astonished. She had thought something really important in the way of news had turned up. Instead here was dear Aunt Dorothy chattering away about parties and the prince regent, as if nothing else mattered. And yet she faced ruin if she did not come to terms with a ruthless blackmailer. How extraordinary the woman was! With a complete lack of deference to her elders, Miranda remembered the exasperation Sir Peter, her father, had sometimes shown toward his only sister. Now she began to understand.

"My dear Miranda, you cannot be attending," said

her aunt. "An invitation to dine with the prince regent. Why even Lady Jersey is rarely honored. It can only mean that Templecombe has asked him to invite us. The prince always takes notice of what he says."

"Oh." At first Miranda could think of nothing else to say. Then she realized that she would have to force her aunt to face up to the problem that confronted them both. "I wish to speak to my aunt for a few moments in private, Miss Dunn," she said somewhat timidly to the formidable dresser.

"Of course, Miss." The reply was full of thwarted curiosity, but Dunn had not been a lady's maid for thirty years without knowing when she must leave the room. Lingering for a moment to make one final adjustment to the pots on the dressing table, she turned on her heel to leave the room.

"That's better," sighed Miranda. "Dear Aunt Dorothy, don't you want to know what happened last night?"

"Of course, I do. Well, I suppose I must, dear Miranda. Only it is so unpleasant to have to think about it," was the reluctant reply. "It upsets me so much that I think I shall fall into a decline. My nerves are not good, as Dr. Lawrence has told me a hundred times. But tell me everything. I must brace myself to know the dreadful truth."

Pouring herself another cup of chocolate, Miranda launched out on her narrative. Her account was not entirely clear, but then she, herself, was far from clear about what it all meant. At the end of the narration, she concluded: "And so I can suppose that the blackmailer must be the Earl of Templecombe."

Lady Eversley, who had been fidgeting with the breakfast-table china throughout Miranda's story, broke into speech. "Templecombe! I cannot believe that, dear

Miranda. I am sure you must be mistaken. I have known him since he was a babe in his mother's arms. Why should he do anything so odious?"

"He is a gambler," offered Miranda. "Sir Samuel tells me that he is desperate for money and is hanging out for a rich wife."

"I cannot believe it all the same," said Lady Eversley. "And surely you did not confide your suspicions to Sir Samuel, Miranda. That would have been most improper."

"No, I didn't explain to him at all why I was even there," said Miranda. "And that in itself was rather embarrassing. I fear he may think I was making an assignation with the earl. But he told me about the earl's gambling habits at my coming-out ball, and I have no reason to suppose he was wrong."

At that moment, Stratton opened the door after a discreet knock. In his hand was a silver salver, and on it a pile of letters. He offered them to Lady Eversley, who took them with dismay.

As he withdrew from the room, Lady Eversley began opening them with trembling hands, and an apprehensive countenance. "Ninety guineas for a reticule? Surely I cannot have paid so much? Madame Latour goes too far with her bills . . . oh, it is the one with the diamond clasp. I suppose it was rather costly. Another invitation, Miranda, see here. It is for Lady Roehampton's conversazione. How tedious. But I suppose we shall have to go for Mr. Martock's sake. Oh dear me." Her chatter ended in a wail. She held out a letter wordlessly to Miranda.

Miranda took it, and looked carefully at the superscription. The writing was the same nondescript but educated hand as the one which had written the blackmail letter of the day before. "This is from the blackmailer, dear

Aunt. Do you want me to open it?" she asked. Lady Eversley nodded nervously.

With an effort, Miranda managed to stop her hands from trembling. Being careful not to tear the paper, she unfolded the sheet.

I am aware that the assignation was kept on Lady Eversley's behalf, but circumstances beyond my control prevented its proper termination. Time will be saved on both sides, if I make clear my demands. For a sum of five thousand guineas, I will undertake to deliver back Lady Eversley's letters. The money must be paid by the end of the month. In a few days I will appoint time and place where it can be handed over.

Miranda read out the letter with amazement. "It is much more specific than the last one," she mused at the end of it. "And the blackmailer has taken to writing in the first person, as if he was no longer afraid so much of detection. What can we make of that? He also knows that the appointment was kept. It must be the earl. Who else could have known that I had come for that purpose?"

She looked round for confirmation at her aunt, and was horrified to see Lady Eversley weeping into her cup of chocolate. *"Five thousand guineas!* I cannot find that sort of sum without selling this house. Lord Eversley left my jointure tied up with all sorts of restrictions. He always said it was to make sure I could manage the money properly. And now I shall be ruined, utterly ruined. Mr. Martock will never marry me, if I have to become bankrupt. And on the same day as Madame Latour charges me an outrageous sum for a reticule!"

At the inconsequence of this last remark, Miranda could not forbear to smile. "You are not ruined yet, Aunt Dorothy," she said cheeringly. "We have till the end of the month to find the money, and perhaps if we can only discover beyond any doubt who the blackmailer is, then we can make a push to get back the letters."

"It is only three weeks," wailed her aunt.

"Please don't cry," said Miranda with an optimism she was far from feeling. "We will manage somehow. You shall marry Mr. Martock. If only I could get my hands on my own money I could lend you the sum."

It was typical of Lady Eversley that she should immediately cheer up at Miranda's words. Her mind moved rapidly on to calculating what economies she could make in her weekly outgoings, so as to find the five thousand guineas. "If we cut down on wax candles. The servants are shockingly extravagant in their use. Perhaps I could persuade Stratton . . ." she mused optimistically. "Or perhaps the answer would be to turn out some of them, but I really do not know whom we could spare. Perhaps one of the kitchen maids could go, but they are bound to be related to the housemaids or something . . . and I suppose Alphonse the chef would leave immediately if I so much as made a *suggestion* about his staff. He is so shockingly temperamental."

Miranda too was thinking hard. "You know, Aunt Dorothy, all this talk of wax candles and servants won't really help us," she said eventually. "The only way that I can see is for me to lend you the money. I certainly can afford to do so. It's too bad that Papa should have tied it all up in that stupid trust. I could ask Mr. Scrimgeour to advance me a loan, but he would be sure to ask what I wanted it for, and I very much doubt whether he would consider that paying off a blackmailer is a proper use for it. If only I was engaged to be married . . ."

"I do not see how that would help," said her aunt. "I am sure you will receive plenty of offers in due course, especially since Templecombe has brought you into fashion. You know, I can't think that he is the blackmailer. I knew his mother. Such a sweet lady, she was." She broke off. "Where was I? Oh yes, dear Miranda, going back to your getting engaged. I am sure you will. But how would it aid us now? You could hardly borrow five thousand guineas from a gentleman, even after getting betrothed."

"No, but according to the family trust, I come into possession of my fortune, to do what I like with it, upon engagement to be married," explained Miranda.

"How extremely odd of my brother," said Lady Eversley, her mind ready to be diverted. "I understand that he should leave the money in trust until your marriage. That is commonplace. But I have never heard of a fortune being tied up until an engagement. What if you were jilted, dear child? Would the money still be yours by right?"

"I imagine so," said Miranda, amused at her aunt's thoughts on the subject. She paused for a moment. "What a fool I am. I never thought of it like that. If I want to lend you the money, all I have to do is engage myself to be married. Then Mr. Scrimgeour will have to make over my fortune, and advance me any sum I choose."

"But who shall you marry, dear Miranda?" asked her aunt doubtfully. "Surely you have not received any offers without letting me know about them. If so, I must tell you it is extremely improper of you."

"No, Aunt Dorothy, have no fear. I have had no offers of marriage—yet," said Miranda. "But do you not see that if only I can get one, then I can become engaged and lend you the money?"

"Three weeks is not very long, Miranda," said her aunt. "And besides, I should not like to think of you marrying somebody you do not care for, just in order to lend me some money. I do not think you have thought what you would be letting yourself in for."

"But you said yourself, Aunt Dorothy, that I did not have to be married to collect the money," argued Miranda. "All I have to do is get myself *engaged* to be married. It is not the same thing. A hundred things could intervene afterward to stop the engagement. Besides, it does not say that it has to be publicly announced. The will simply mentioned a betrothal. It did not specify an announcement in *The Gazette* or anything."

"I suppose it might work," said her aunt doubtfully. "But who do you think would come up to scratch so quickly?"

"Sir Samuel Brassey might," offered Miranda. "He seemed awfully keen at the ball. Do you remember, he said he would call on us."

Her aunt's face brightened. "Sir Samuel Brassey. What a wonderful idea, Miranda," she said. "Such a nice man. Such exquisite manners. And he's so rich. Not that I think for a moment that you are interested in such things, Miranda, but he lives in a very lavish way and it is undeniable, my dear, that his wife could expect every comfort. I am so glad that he is a favorite of yours. There is only one drawback. Let us be frank about it. His birth. Nobody quite knows very much about his family, but there is no doubting that he is very eligible. Why, Diana Hatfield has been on the catch for him these past few weeks."

"He is not exactly a favorite of mine," said Miranda carefully. "But I suppose he would do. I am obliged to him for rescuing me last night. I was excessively glad to see him . . ." She recollected the embarrassing moment when the earl—that hateful beast, she thought—had taken her in his arms. At the memory she blushed.

Lady Eversley saw the blush, and gave a little trill of laughter. "You naughty puss, Miranda," she said. "I am sure Sir Samuel would make a very good husband indeed. He has nothing but that poor cousin of his looking after him at the moment. Jennifer Brassey is a nobody of a woman and I am sure he would be very pleased to pension her off as soon as possible. Of course, now I come to think of it, Sir Samuel's arrival last night was excessively romantic."

Miranda didn't quite know what to say. She felt she could not embark on long and even more embarrassing explanations. And perhaps her aunt was right. Sir Samuel *would* make a very good husband. He was rich, and good-looking, and everybody agreed he had charming manners. But something about him frightened her. . . . She mentally gave herself a shake and told herself not to be silly. Getting engaged to Sir Samuel was the best scheme yet to deal with the blackmailer, and perhaps only Sir Samuel could protect them both against the earl.

At this auspicious moment in the conversation, Miss Dunn knocked at the door and announced: "Sir Samuel has called, my lady. I have shown him into the morning room and told him that I will see if you can come down."

"So early," said Lady Eversley in a tone of irritation. Then she brightened. "He must be excessively eager to see you, Miranda dear. Shall you go down and tell him I will be a little moment or two?"

"I would prefer not." Miranda blushed. She did not wish to talk to Sir Samuel without the moral support of her aunt.

"Quite right, my dear." Lady Eversley nodded approvingly. "Well, I shall make a hurried toilet. Dunn, you must help me. I know my hair is quite unfit to be seen, but my presence is needed down below. Stay here, Miranda dear, while I dress. It seems shocking to be in such a hurry, but we must not keep the lover waiting."

Such remarks were not to Miranda's taste, but she was thankful that her aunt had not sent her downstairs to entertain Sir Samuel, and so held her tongue. Nevertheless it was in a blushing and self-conscious way she entered the morning room in her aunt's train. Sir Samuel marked her expression, she felt, but gave no outward sign other than a norrowing of the eyes. He bowed with dandified grace over their hands.

He was exquisitely dressed, as ever, this time for riding. His white buckskin breeches were as tight as pantaloons, and not the shadow of a stain interrupted their brilliance. His boots gleamed in such a way as to make Miranda think his valet must have used blacking mixed with champagne to get such an effect. They were graced with white tops of the kind Beau Brummell had made famous. A faultless but plain cravat tied in an Osbaldeston knot graced his neck. The same large ruby pin that he had worn with his evening clothes glimmered among its folds. On a lesser man it might have looked vulgar, but Miranda had to admit that Sir Samuel carried it off with an air. The same ruby ring was on his finger, though he carried a pair of tan gloves.

"Forgive my unsuitable clothes for paying a morning call," he was apologizing to Lady Eversley. "I have come in the hope that Miss Melbury may consent to accompany me riding in the park."

There was nothing in his manner to distinguish between the two ladies on whom he was calling, except a certain smile that hovered around his thin lips as his eyes met those of Miranda. She remembered the hot wet kiss he had placed in the palm of her hand the night before, and felt slightly uncomfortable.

"I do not know whether it is suitable for me to accompany you, Sir Samuel," said Miranda primly to cover her confusion.

"I am hoping to tempt you beyond all doubt," he replied with a widening smile. "I have the most lovely little mare outside for you. If you look out of the window you will see she is the most delightful little creature. Not up to the magnificence of the stallion, Diabolo, was it? that you were telling me about at the ball. But I am sure you will approve of her."

Miranda went to the window. There in the street a groom was walking up and down with a truly delightful gray Arab mare. She could not help showing her enthusiastic approval in her expression. "She is a nice little thing," she said to the Beau. "I must congratulate you on your choice of horseflesh."

"It is the mare I bought for my cousin Jennifer," said Sir Samuel. "I told her the night of the ball that my cousin is too poor spirited to ride her. There is not an ounce of vice in the mare, but she is a little hot to handle. Miss Melbury would be doing me a favor by exercising her."

"I do not know whether, as a conscientious aunt, I can give my permission," said Lady Eversley doubtfully. "It is not at all the thing for my niece to accompany you by herself, Sir Samuel. It looks so peculiar."

"I have come prepared for this eventuality. If you look again, Miss Melbury, you will see that that my cousin awaits outside, too," said Sir Samuel. "She will surely be adequate as a chaperone, Lady Eversley."

"Is Miss Brassey out there by herself? Sir Samuel, you should have brought her in. I would not for the world be so impolite as not to offer her some refreshment. It is quite shocking to leave her outside on her horse. She must come in at once. I shall have the pleasure of a few minutes' conversation with her, while Miranda changes into her riding habit."

Miranda glanced toward Lady Eversley in a questioning way, and her aunt nodded. With the addition of the colorless Miss Jennifer Brassey, riding in the park with a gentleman was unexceptionable. Miranda was both glad and sorry. She was itching to ride the lovely little mare, but at the same time she felt an odd reluctance to be with Sir Samuel. Still, she thought, the presence of Miss Brassey must guard me against any embarrassing importunities.

As she was dressing for riding, another thought struck her. How odd of Sir Samuel to have left Miss Brassey outside, for all the world as if she was a dog to be kept out of the way until her master wanted her. It did not seem a kind of thing to do. For the first time Miranda wondered if Miss Brassey was happy living with her cousin.

A mere ten minutes later, she reappeared in the drawing room. She was wearing one of the riding habits that Sir Peter had procured for his only daughter from a London tailor. It was one of the few garments she had brought with her to London that had met with her aunt's total approval, being fashionably cut and completely à la mode. Called a Glengarry habit, it was of pale blue cloth, richly ornamented with frogs and braiding in a manner so as to define her slender figure to considerable advantage. A habit shirt of soft cambric, with a high-standing lace-trimmed collar, a cravat of soft muslin, and lace ruffles at the sleeves softened the severity of the habit itself. A Glengarry cap of blue satin, trimmed with ribbon and a cheeky plume of blue feathers completed the dashing toilette.

"You look a positive Diana of the chase," breathed Sir Samuel. His eyes lingered appreciatively on the vision she presented.

"A very becoming habit, I am sure," murmured Miss Brassey in acidulated tones.

Miranda found her temper rising. Try as she would, she could not like Miss Brassey.

Miss Brassey could not be condemned for being overfashionable. Her riding habit was soberly cut in some kind of dull brown material, and she looked little disposed to enjoy a ride. Miranda noticed, as polite conversation was carried on for a few minutes, that Miss Brassy rarely took much part in what was being said. If she did make some remark, she looked to Sir Samuel for guidance and confirmation, as if she was anxious not to offend even by so much as a few words.

"The mare is almost as high-spirited and as beautiful as Miss Melbury, herself," the Beau was saying. "Indeed, her high spirits are a little too much for Jennifer. I daresay that had I broken her myself I might have made a better job of her, for she is rather a handful for a lady's hack. Not too much for Miss Melbury, I will wager, of course."

"Do you break your own horses, then, Sir Samuel?" asked Miranda with some surprise. She had somehow thought he was too much the London man of fashion to go in for such pursuits. "I have had a hand in breaking horses myself. Helmslow, my groom, always believes in training his own young 'uns, if he can. But I sometimes think it is a sad business to take a young colt, so wild and so free, and make it obedient to the human's whim."

"I always have believed that most horses are happier once they have been fastened," said the Beau with a silky smile. "Though they do not know it, they need the curb and bit. Their own nature demands it." He flicked an imaginary piece of dust from his faultless riding jacket, and with a change of voice said to Lady Eversley: "With your permission, I shall take Miss Melbury in the park. It is a lovely day for riding, and I am anxious for her to try out the mare's paces."

As they left the house, Miranda felt oddly apprehensive. It was nothing to do with the little Arab mare, whom she no sooner mounted than she discovered had a beautifully light mouth and excellent paces. For a minute or two, the high-spirited little horse showed off its *joie de vivre* with a tiny flick of its heels and half-rear. Lady Eversley regarded this from the steps of number 100 Eaton Square with dismay, but she had to acknowledge that Miranda seemed completely at home. With the lightest of pressure on the reins, and no use of her riding crop at all, she brought the mare under control. With dancing steps they made their way to Rotten Row.

As they broke into a canter down the Row, Miranda's feeling of fear disappeared. It was such a lovely day, and the mare was such a delightful ride. The Row was quite crowded with riders, carriages, and walkers. All the fashionable world seemed to be there and the lively scene contrasted with its deserted darkness the night before.

After a few moments, Miranda realized that Miss Brassey and the groom that had accompanied them seemed to have fallen behind. "I fear that your cousin is mounted on a fearful slug of a hack," she said to the Beau, who was beside her on what she noticed was a magnificent, if nervous, chestnut. "I feel guilty at riding her delightful little mare."

"My cousin has fallen behind on my instructions," said Sir Samuel. "After our encounter last night, Miss Melbury, I felt the need for private conversation with you."

"Oh," said Miranda, none too pleased. "You know, Sir Samuel," she carried on, collecting her courage, "I do hope you do not think ill of me because of that encounter. It may have looked like a midnight assignation, but I do assure you that the Earl of Templecombe is the last man on earth toward whom I feel tender emotions."

"I am glad to hear it, Miss Melbury," said Sir Samuel. "I was desperately anxious lest you had lost your heart to a gambler and a rake. As I remember, you are fond of moonlight and you felt a stroll in the park would be romantic." His voice was mocking.

She wished now that she had not invented such an obviously weak story. "What I should like to make clear," she persevered, "is that I was not expecting to see the Earl of Templecombe." That at least was true, she reflected. She had not for a moment imagined that he could have been the blackmailer.

"You relieve my mind of its burdens. I should not have liked to think that you have fallen prey to a man like that," said Sir Samuel. "It is not for one gentleman to speak ill of another, but I was anxious about your innocence, Miss Melbury. It is the chief of your charms, as far as I am concerned. Templecombe is a practiced charmer, and it was widely talked about, the way he had singled you out at your coming-out ball. I should not like to feel that you were going to be like the other young ladies he has ruined."

"Ruined?" Miranda could not help showing her surprise. "That is a strong word, Sir Samuel. Are you sure?"

"Perhaps it *is* rather a strong word, Miss Melbury," admitted the Beau by her side. "Let us say that the Earl of Templecombe is often seen with a wide variety of ladies who do not come from the highest ranks of society. He is known for his opera dancers, his *petites amies,* and, not to put too fine a point on it, he has kept some of the most ravishing mistresses in London. Till now his interests have centered only on those young women who do not belong in your world, Miss Melbury. Then when he showed his fascination with you, I was seriously concerned. I do know that I should not be saying such things openly to you, but I thought it was best to know about his reputation."

Miranda hardly knew how to reply. She was aware that this was a very improper conversation, and yet by her conduct in being seen embraced by the Earl of Templecombe in the darkness of the park, she had in a sense given Sir Samuel the right to talk about such things. In one way she found the man beside her impressive. He was beautifully dressed and equally beautifully mounted. Miranda had to admire his judgement of horseflesh, even though she had noticed, and felt disapproval of the fact, that he was wearing runnelled spurs. Already that chesnut he was riding had a speck of blood on his flanks. Yet spurs were common to many riders. She could not really blame him for following custom, she supposed.

"Do you disapprove of me, Sir Samuel," she said, trying with a light touch to turn the conversation. "I hope I have not sunk myself below reproach in my foolish conduct, searching out the moonlight last night."

"Miss Melbury, I find you as exquisite and as high-spirited as, shall we say, the mare you are riding. How can I prove my devotion? I would love to do so. Anything I have is yours to command."

This was a reply with a vengeance. Miranda was uncertain if he was mocking her or being serious. She was thinking hard. She needed an offer of marriage, as surely no girl had ever done so before. Might she trust this man by her side? She took a deep breath. "Might I ask you, upon your honor and all you hold dearest, not to reveal to a soul what I am going to say to you?"

"I hold my honor dearest of all things," he said grandly. "I swear on it that what you say will be secret between us."

"Well," she said haltingly, "I have decided that . . . that I do not care very much for being an unattached young lady. I have decided . . ." it was extraordinarily difficult to say what she meant, "that I would feel happier if there was somebody . . . somebody to whom I was attached, to whom I could turn . . ."

"Miss Melbury, might I help you? Would you do me the honor of thinking of me as that person?" Sir Samuel came to her rescue with commendable promptness. "Might I approach Lady Eversley and ask her permission to pay my addresses in a formal manner to you? If you would become . . ." he paused for just a split second, "my wife, I should be most honored."

Miranda cantered on with a terrible feeling of gloom. She had what she needed—an offer of marriage. Yet she was overwhelmed, not with relief, but with fear. Had she done the right thing? There was hardly any point in thinking about it. She could hardly back out now.

"Your offer of marriage comes as a surprise," she said untruthfully and idiotically. "I hardly know how to answer you, Sir Samuel." She looked at him for the first time and saw that his expression was one of growing anger. "But I do appreciate your kindness," she went on hurriedly. "I should like it if you would talk to Lady Eversley. I should . . . should be happy to be your wife."

Sir Samuel's expression changed from anger to pleasure. "You have made me very happy, Miranda darling."

His use of her first name gave Miranda rather a shock, until she realized that it was quite reasonable on the lips of the man she had contracted to marry. "If we were not so uncomfortably placed on separate horses, I should demonstrate my happiness in a warmer manner," he said softly, with one of his silky smiles.

Miranda was conscious of a feeling of relief that she *was* mounted. She felt unreasonably shy. To cheer herself, she thought of the horrid fate hanging over her aunt. At least Lady Eversley would be delighted at the news. Not only would it offer a chance for her to pay off the blackmailer, but it would also please her as a very suitable match. "It seems so odd to think of marriage," she said somewhat inconsequently to the Beau. "I am not sure if I am ready for it."

"Have no doubt, my beauty," said Sir Samuel. "I know when a mare needs gentle handling. I shall be gentle with you."

She shuddered, and she thought that he noticed. But if he did, it did not worry him, for his smile stayed on his face. If anything, it seemed stronger than before. "Only, there is one thing," she said. "You will not tell anybody else yet, will you, Sir Samuel? I should not care yet for all the congratulations and the fuss that will be made."

"I shall tell my cousin, Miranda darling, and of course your aunt. It would not be possible to conceal it from either." Then as he saw a flicker of fear pass over her face, he added: "But, if you prefer not, we shall not tell the rest of the world. How I shall laugh at the young men who besiege you for dancing, knowing that you are mine alone, promised to me, and belonging one day utterly to me!" He gave a low laugh. In Miranda's ears it sounded almost a gloating laugh.

"Thank you, Sir Samuel," is all she said, however. "Perhaps you would add to your kindness. I am naturally rather . . . shy about this. Would you take it on yourself to talk to Lady Eversley on your return? I will leave you with her."

Sir Samuel fell smoothly in with her wishes, and with a delicacy she would not have credited him with, talked of other subjects for the rest of their ride. He told her of the race horses that ran under his colors, and Miranda had to acknowledge that he seemed knowledgeable about horses, even if something told her that he did not *care* for them in quite the way she did.

Back at Eaton Square, she found herself for a moment alone with Miss Brassey. Sir Samuel was giving instructions to the groom about the disposal of the mare she was riding. "I hope we shall get to know each other better, Miss Brassey," she said politely to the older woman, feeling that some sort of kind word should be spoken. After all, even if she might not marry Sir Samuel, she was going to be *betrothed* to him. That argued kindness to his relative.

"Thank you, Miss Melbury," said Miss Brassey rather shortly. "I don't suppose we shall. I do not usually know Sir Samuel's friends very well. I don't care to mix too much in very fashionable circles."

In the face of what seemed evident hostility, Miranda did not know what to say. Murmuring something about having enjoyed the ride, she dismounted from the mare, and took the chance of patting its glossy neck to avoid further talk.

Back in the house, she went hurriedly to her room, bidding Sir Samuel and Miss Brassey rather perfunctory goodbyes and thanks. She was anxious to avoid another *tête à tête* with him. As she took off her riding habit with the help of her maid, and put on a muslin day dress made in a deceptively simple style by one of the extremely expensive dressmakers patronized by Lady Eversley, she wondered if she had done the right thing. Getting engaged to be married to Sir Samuel seemed such a desperate move to make. And yet it would undoubtedly solve the problem of how to find five thousand guineas. Mr. Scrimgeour would have to advance her the sum now, and he would no doubt think it was for the purchase of a trousseau or some such object relating to the wedding. The wedding . . . Miranda trembled at the thought. Well, nothing said that she had to get married, just because she was engaged to be married. Of course, it would cause talk. But perhaps Sir Samuel would jilt her.

Cautiously waiting until she heard the front door shut on Sir Samuel and his cousin, she went down to meet her aunt.

Lady Eversley greeted her with enthusiasm, embracing her and kissing her on both cheeks. "I am so happy for you, Miranda. Sir Samuel is such a charming man, and I am sure that you will have everything you want, married to him. Such great wealth, such charm, such exquisite manners . . . I wish you could have heard him asking for your hand just now! It was enough to make me want to cry. And such talk of how you had inherited my beauty . . . Flattery, I told him, of course."

Miranda hardly knew what to say. Her aunt was treating the whole transaction as if it was a love match, instead of an engagement of convenience. She wondered whether to remind her that the whole point of it all was to get Mr. Scrimgeour to advance five thousand guineas, but decided not to. Poor Aunt Dorothy probably just couldn't face the thought. If it comforted her to pretend that her niece's engagement was part of a romance, well, then perhaps she must be allowed that comfort. Not for the first time Miranda found herself thinking of her aunt as if *she* was the young child who must be protected and indulged.

5

Only a little time after that momentous ride in the Park with Beau Brassey, Lady Eversley had received another visitor, Mr. James Martock. He called very correctly in the afternoon, at a time when the ladies were recruiting their strength after a light luncheon.

To the ordinary eye of the household servant there was nothing special about his call. Mr. Martock was in the habit of calling upon Lady Eversley. He was a regular visitor at 100 Eaton Square.

Mr. Martock was dressed with his normal propriety that afternoon, in a pair of Petersham pantaloons of a sober dark brown color. His cravat was tied plainly in a simple style that proclaimed he did not aspire to the heights of fashion. His beaver hat was high at the crown, but a good two or three inches lower than those of younger men.

Despite his lack of fashionable aspirations, Mr. Martock was popular among Lady Eversley's household staff, from his habit of slipping a silver shilling into the palm of the footman who took his beaver hat and tan gloves. He was popular too with Stratton, the butler, whose apparently impassive gaze missed little of importance. Stratton had looked at Mr. Martock and drawn his own conclusions that here was a man very much in love with his mistress, Lady Eversley. He therefore favored Mr. Martock with an indulgent, "Good afternoon, sir. It is a nice day for calling," and showed him straight into the salon where he would find the two ladies sitting over the romances they had taken out from the circulating library. After doing this, Stratton went in search of the best claret. A man in love, in the butler's view, needed to keep up his strength, and what better refreshment than the best claret that the Eaton Square cellars could afford.

Inside the salon Lady Eversley sprang rather nervously to her feet. "Dear Mr. Martock, what a pleasure to see you! I hope you like Miranda's new dress from Latour. The threadwork on the bodice is ravishing, don't you think? If only I was not so horrifyingly old, I vow I would have one made up exactly like it."

"You become whatever you wear, Lady Eversley," said Mr. Martock with rather ponderous gallantry. He turned to Miranda and obligingly tried to think of a suitable remark to make on her new dress. "Your aunt is right, Miss Melbury. The dress looks very fine on you this morning," he managed.

"Thank you, Mr. Martock," said Miranda, curtseying. On his entrance, she had determined to take a hand in the affair between him and Lady Eversley. Dear Aunt Dorothy, it was clear, was fond of the man, and there was no doubt in Miranda's mind that the very best thing would be if she would confide in him. She decided she would leave them alone together, no matter how odd it looked. "I hope you will excuse me, Mr. Martock," she said unconvincingly but firmly. "It is important that I speak to Dunn for a moment."

She whisked herself to the door and out of the room before her aunt could think up any remark that might stop her. As she shut the door, she heaved a sigh of relief. Now was Lady Eversley's chance.

"I am so sorry that Miranda has gone off in that very odd way," apologized Lady Eversley, more than a little rattled by her niece's abrupt departure.

"It is you I have come to see, Lady Eversley, not Miranda, though I own I find the girl charming," said Mr. Martock. He looked at her with a serious gaze.

Her ladyship laughed a tinkling laugh out of nervousness. "A compliment from you, Mr. Martock?" she said archly. "Wonders will never cease. You are usually so solemn that I must not look for pretty speeches." She paused hopefully.

Mr. Martock declined the gambit. His serious turn of mind was just a little bit offended by her ladyship's tone. "When I am with you, I always mean to make pretty speeches," he said in explanation, "but I cannot think of them. I hope that my lack of easy compliments will not stand against my interest with you, Lady Eversley." There was a pause. Mr. Martock ploughed on. "I am anxious to be of service to you, Lady Eversley. I would lift off your shoulders all the burdens and cares of widowhood, if I could, Lady Eversley."

What ails the man? thought Lady Eversley crossly. Not for the first time she felt a pang of irritation at her lover's serious nature. But there was no doubt that whatever his words, he meant well. She decided to see if she could not work the conversation round so that she might be able to tell him of her major burden and care at the moment—the blackmailing letters.

"Dear Mr. Martock. I shall have no hesitation in

telling you that there are burdens and cares that I face, and that I find it difficult to deal with them as a woman on my own," she said.

She was about to continue in greater detail, when, unfelicitously, Mr. Martock interrupted her. "I can imagine those cares" he said soothingly. "Why, even my sister, Lady Roehampton, finds it difficult to live alone. My dear, I must tell you how high an opinion she holds of you. She told me only the other day that she considered you were preeminent for virtue and discretion."

A shadow of annoyance crossed Lady Eversley's face. Lady Roehampton, a fussy, stuffy woman if ever there was one, was not a favorite with her. Indeed, she was the only thing that made Lady Eversley wonder whether she ought to marry Mr. Martock. Having a sister-in-law who was forever going on about good works and virtue would be a terrible bore. But unfortunately Mr. Martock thought the world of his elder sister.

"Dear Lady Roehampton," cooed Lady Eversley, concealing her desire to tell Mr. Martock just what she thought of his only sister, "how kind of her to say such nice things. And yet, Mr. Martock, I fear I have not always been so wise as I might have been . . ." She started again to try and work the conversation round to a point from which she might confess her real problem.

"You are wisdom itself," said Mr. Martock fervently and foolishly.

Lady Eversley sighed. This was being difficult. "There is something which is worrying me a great deal, and I feel sure I can trust you . . ." she tried again.

A knock at the door stopped her continuing. It was Stratton with the Margaux and the special glasses. "I took the liberty of bringing a glass of claret for Mr. Martock," he said in his expressionless voice.

"Thank you, Stratton," said Lady Eversley helplessly.

The butler bowed himself out of the door, confident that he had done all he could to make the path of true love smooth. Had he known that his interference had prevented an important confidence, he would have been much mortified. As it was, he retreated to the housekeeper's room, there to discuss with Mrs. Jones the prospects of their mistress changing her state of life. No rumor was allowed to escape to the housemaids and footmen who would be equally interested. Such a delicate matter was kept entirely from the inferior household staff. Time enough for them to learn when the match had been properly concluded.

In the salon, Lady Eversley had given up her attempts to raise the ugly little matter of her letters to Mr. Ambrose. It was clear that Mr. Martock, kind and good man that he was, was so utterly besotted that he did not associate her with even the slightest imperfection. Raising the matter of blackmail, she feared, might give his infant love its death blow. Vaguely, she thought, perhaps somehow he need not know.

So when Miranda returned to the salon after nearly half an hour, she failed to find what she had hoped—a happy and confiding couple. Mr. Martock was still being gallant and in love, to be sure. Lady Eversley was being kind and welcoming to his attentions. But there had obviously been no confidence between the two of them.

Her arrival seemed to stir Lady Eversley out of her lethargy. "My dearest wish is to see Miranda happily settled," said Lady Eversley in a teasing tone of voice. "That may be not far off, Mr. Martock. But I will say no more on the topic unless Miranda gives me leave." She looked inquiringly at her niece.

"I would prefer you not to mention my plans for the

moment," said Miranda quietly. At this stage she did not want to discuss her engagement with Mr. Martock. If only Lady Eversley had seized the opportunity, which she, Miranda, had given her, to discuss the matter with Mr. Martock, thought Miranda. Then perhaps she need not engage herself to Sir Samuel Brassey. Somehow she felt particularly anxious and melancholy about the scheme. While she had been leaving her two elders alone together, she had written a letter to Mr. Scrimgeour, requesting five thousand guineas as soon as possible on the strength of her engagement to be married to Sir Samuel Brassey. It had not been an easy letter to write.

There was a moment's silence. Then, to Miranda's relief, Mr. Martock rose from the Chesterfield sofa where he had been sitting. "I must take my leave, Lady Eversley," he said. "I am visiting the Duke of Wellington this afternoon, to beg him to give my nephew a cornetsy in cavalry. Lady Roehampton feels that her younger son Charley is a little wild, and that the military life may be of benefit to him."

"You are so kind to your sister," said Lady Eversley. There was just the slightest hint of disapproval in the remark.

"I cannot fail to remember her kindness to me when I was a child, and she was my elder," said Mr. Martock gravely. "I have an obligation to help her now that she is a widow and needs my support. It is not easy to be a woman alone in the world."

"Oh, I know, I know only too well." Lady Eversley spoke feelingly. The way she said the words made it clear to Miranda that her aunt had not confided in Mr. Martock. There was no denying that this was a blow. She had so hoped that Aunt Dorothy might have found the courage to confess all.

Her aunt saw Mr. Martock from the room. She came back looking rather shamefaced. "I just could not tell him, Miranda. I tried, really I tried. But he kept talking about that boring Lady Roehampton and I could not bring myself . . . He thinks I am wise and discreet, and I am nothing of the kind."

Miranda sighed. "It is more urgent than ever before," she said, as much to herself as to her aunt. "I have written to Mr. Scrimgeour, telling him of my engagement, and asking him for the money immediately. But I have a strong suspicion that he will try to delay paying out the money as long as possible."

"There are only two or three weeks left till the end of the month," Lady Eversley wrung her hands as she thought of it. "And, say what you will, Miranda, I do not think Mr. Martock would continue to love me if those letters were shown to him."

Miranda flung herself down on the Chesterfield and put her head in her hands. She was thinking hard, desperately hard. "What would the blackmailer do, if he came across more letters?" she asked.

"There aren't any more letters," said Lady Eversley, affronted. "I don't make a habit of writing such things, Miranda. It was just that Philip Ambrose was so sweet and gentle that I forgot myself."

"I know there aren't any more letters," said Miranda impatiently. "But the blackmailer doesn't know that. Suppose he was offered some more letters. He would surely want to get his hands on them, would he not?"

"I suppose so. But I do not understand how that would help us. It would only make the situation very much worse."

"Do you not see, dear Aunt, that our main problem is that we cannot be sure that the Earl of Templecombe *is* the blackmailer? There was no opportunity for this when I encountered him in the park, and it seems to me that until we can be absolutely *sure,* there is very little we can do. But once we know for certain that it was he, why then perhaps we could find some way of putting pressure upon him to give up those letters. Now if I was to disguise myself, and to offer him some more letters of yours, then surely, if he is the blackmailer, he would try to purchase these. Then we should know about him, and he would have incriminated himself beyond all doubt."

There was silence for a while while Lady Eversley worked out what Miranda was suggesting. "I still cannot believe it is the earl," she complained, "But I suppose you are right. We must try to discover beyond any doubt. If he is the blackmailer, then he will want the letters. But, Miranda, suppose for an instant that he is not? My reputation will be in shreds, surely?"

"I shall have to be careful in what I say," said Miranda firmly. "If I offer the letters in a guarded fashion, then it should not be obvious what they really are. If he understands too quickly, why, then he must be the blackmailer. If not, then he will probably put me down as a servant who has lost his place and is trying for revenge."

After a few more objections from Lady Eversley, the plan was agreed on. "After all," said Lady Eversley thoughtfully, "I dare not bring Mr. Martock to the point of making an offer until this threat is no longer hanging over me. It is horrible to think that it is the Earl of Templecombe behind it all, but the more I consider the matter the more I realize that you *must* be right. Who else can it be? I cannot think why I ever thought he was so charming. He is nothing but a ruthless debauché."

Miranda found herself wishing to interrupt. She discovered that she was utterly perverse. When her aunt insisted that the earl was innocent, she had been anxious to persuade her otherwise. Not that she had succeeded, she had an absurd impulse to spring to his defense when her aunt criticized him.

Upstairs, she rummaged fiercely through the chest of drawers in her bedchamber, pulling out huge heaps of finery—silk stockings, lace handkerchiers, bodices, petticoats, shawls and other fripperies. Right at the bottom of all this she found what she wanted—a pair of men's riding breeches and a jacket.

They looked more disgraceful than she had remembered, and as she gazed on them they took her memory forcibly back to her old life, "I was free then" she mused, thinking of the way she and her father would set out on their horses for a day's hacking round the estate. Miranda had not realized just how unusually she had been brought up until now. In the light of her new life in fashionable London, she had begun to wonder whether it had been such a good thing. Sir Peter, balked of the son and heir he must have wanted, had made for himself the next best thing, a tomboy of a daughter. Had it been entirely wise?

She wriggled into the garments, which had already become a little tight for her. She smiled at the thought of what Miss Dunn would say, if she saw her now. Looking in the mirror, she carefully disarranged her fashionable curls, making them tangle in such a way as a street urchin's locks might.

Staring into the glass, she thought she made quite a good boy. The ladylike curves that were developing on her, were not evidence under the jacket. Thank goodness, too, that short curls were the mode. All she needed now was her travelling cloak to cover up the shocking garments so that she could leave the house without scandalising the servants.

The breeches were essential to her plan. If the Earl Templecombe was not to recognize her, he must not associate her with the young girl he had danced with only a few nights ago, or met, dressed in her sober grey, in the párk at night. Of course there was the danger he might recognize her, being dressed in the same garments that she had been on their first encounter. But Miranda thought this was slight. She would conceal her voice, rub dirt into her face, and generally put on all the gestures of an urchin. She was confident she could carry it off.

But this confidence was shaken when she arrived at the earl's townhouse in Grosvenor Square. She had borrowed her aunt's town coach, a slightly cumberous vehicle, but one which provided privacy. Helmslow accompanied her at her request. For once he did not question her, contenting himself with sitting well back on the coach's leather cushions and smoking his pipe. Miranda could feel his unspoken disapproval throughout the journey, but his presence was a comfort nonetheless.

When Lady Eversley had asked her whether she was sure she could trust him, she had replied: "Oh yes, I would trust him with my life. After all, he put me on my first pony."

Lady Eversley had not thought that the act of placing a young child on its first pony (surely a hazardous proceeding) was such proof of trustworthiness. But she had held her tongue, knowing from past experience with her brother, Sir Peter, that those who were horsemad held inexplicable beliefs connected with their favorite pursuit. "Take care, Miranda," she had merely said. "And for heaven's sake, make sure that the earl doesn't recognize you, else we shall both be ruined."

Outside the earl's imposing front door, that possibility suddenly seemed much more likely than it had in Lady

Eversley's salon. For the first time it occurred to Miranda, as she waited for a moment in the coach, that she might have difficulty even in getting into see the earl. High-class butlers, she belatedly realized, were not in the habit of letting unknown ragamuffins in by the front door when the servants' entrance would be so much more appropriate.

Luck favored, however. For just as she stood hesitating at the bottom of the steps, a tall figure was let out of the house. The immaculate blue Celeste coat, tailored by Weston, of course, could only belong to one man, the Earl of Templecombe. A buff-colored waistcoat and a deep stiff white cravat, with buckskin breeches and glowing Hessians were the rest of his attire.

"Please, Sir. It is of the utmost importance that I speak to you about a private matter concerning your lordship," said Miranda in boyish tones with a country accent. She touched her forlock in a respectful manner.

The earl paused and looked down at her. "What do you want with me, boy?"

"I have information concerning Lady Eversley," she replied.

Very deliberately he withdrew a quizzing glass from his waistcoat pocket. In silence he examined her through the glass. "Then you'd best go to Lady Eversley," he said in a drawling voice.

"Please, your honor, it is private information which I believe will interest *you*," Miranda tried again. The earl was still scrutinizing her with his quizzing glass and she felt very uncomfortable. His stern eyes seemed to bore through her disguise, and Miranda would have trembled, had she dared. Instead she tried to stand there carelessly like any boy might.

"Come with me, boy," he said suddenly. He led the way back up the steps. As if by magic, the door was opened by an imposing butler, and silently the earl gestured for him to lead the way into a room adjoining the hall. Not a flicker of emotion betrayed this servant's amazement at his master's strange companion.

"You will leave us, Fields," said the earl as they entered the room. The door was closed silently behind them.

The earl flung himself carelessly down on a chair, leaving Miranda to stand in front of him. "Now, boy, why do you want to see me?" he said grimly.

Miranda's heart sank. This was the moment she had been waiting for, a moment which should have made her feel exhilarated. At last she was in front of the man who had been responsible for the blackmailing letters. If he had been entirely innocent, he would never have invited a mere ragamuffin into the house. The man sitting idly in front of her, swinging his quizzing glass on its chain, was guilty. She had supposed that finding out for sure would have been rather a relief, for it at least meant that she and Aunt Dorothy knew with whom they had to contend. But a sick feeling of depression was all she felt now.

"I have some letters, my lord, which may interest you. Not here with me, but I know where they can be found. I am anxious to place the letters in proper hands."

"I might be interested in these letters," said the earl slowly. "I will see them, if you please."

"I don't think you quite understand," went on Miranda. "I must be compensated for them. It has been very costly to get them."

"How much?" drawled the earl.

"A hundred guineas," she said, naming a sum that might be thought a fortune by a street boy.

"A hundred guineas," mused the earl. He got up from his chair and went over to a desk which stood against the wall. "A hundred guineas is a lot of money," he said, as he pulled out a drawer and, to Miranda's surprise, began counting out a pile of gold. She had not thought that he would part from his money so soon. He walked back toward her, and handed over several gold coins. "And now, Miss Melbury," he said in an unaltered voice, "perhaps you would tell me what this masquerade is all about."

Miranda jumped. She was shattered. She stood there, her mouth gaping with astonishment. He had seen through her. What on earth could she say to him now? Why had he led her on in this way? How was she going to explain her conduct.

"You must indeed be wondering," she said shakily, trying to play for time.

"I think it damned strange," he said with bitter emphasis. "You must think me a fool, Miss Melbury. I recognized you in the street. Did you think that I would not? Why, if I am not mistaken, those are the very same breeches you wore when I first encountered you. I think I am entitled to an explanation of this outrageous conduct, do you not agree?"

His earlier use of the term "masquerade" had given Miranda an idea. She gave what she hoped was a careless tinkle of laughter. "Fie, Lord Templecombe," she said, trying for a flirtatious tone, "you are monstrously cross. It was only a wager I had bet that I could not disguize myself. It is too bad that you have recognized me. I was confident that you would not."

The earl glared at her. "May I ask with whom this disreputable wager has been struck?" he asked unpleasantly.

"Sir Samuel Brassey," said Miranda. As soon as she said the name, she knew it was a terrible mistake. It had just popped into her mouth without her giving it thought. She tried to put it right. "Please don't mention the subject to him," she said. "It was entirely my idea, and he does not know that I have taken him at his word. It was merely that in careless conversation he bet me that I could not conceal my identity. I wagered that I could, even from somebody as perspicacious as yourself."

"I suppose this remarkable and very unsuitable wager took place while you were riding with him in Rotten Row," sneered the earl. "When I saw you encouraging his attentions, I had little idea that you would go to these lengths to fulfill some sordid bet you had made with him. What have you wagered? A kiss? Or do you only bet for real gold, Miss Melbury? Is money what excites your interest?"

Miranda stood dumbly before him. She could not defend herself without going into explanations that would involve Lady Eversley. All she could do was keep silent and let the storm break over her head.

The earl had not finished with her. "Oh don't fear, Miss Melbury. I shall not mention the matter to Sir Samuel. Even he might think it a little too much for you to go gallivanting around dressed like a guttersnipe. I should not like to interfere with any interest you may have there. But tell me one thing. What gave you the idea of offering me old letters of Lady Eversley's? This aspect of your little joke has escaped me."

"I do not wish to speak of it, Lord Templecombe," said Miranda, her head held low. She could not look him in the face. With an effort she made herself say, "I hope that perhaps you can forget this episode. I offer you my humble apologies."

"I shall certainly do my best to forget it," was the deliberate response from the earl. "I am at a loss why you should in the first place have picked me to play pranks upon. I should have thought that your earlier experience might have made it clear to you what I think of women who wear breeches."

She said nothing.

"Oh yes," said the earl, "I will not mention this again, but if by any chance, Miss Melbury, you are considering *selling* your aunt's correspondence, I should think again. I can ruin you, and I shall have no hesitation in doing so, should I see fit. I have only to tell Fields the true identity of the guttersnipe he let in the house, and give him leave to tell his cronies in 'The Running Footman.' I do not think your credit would survive such a devastating story as that one."

"I was not really trying to sell my aunt's letters. There are no such letters," said Miranda desperately. "It was just that I had to have an excuse for a boy off the streets wishing to see you privately."

From his expression, he obviously did not believe a word of what she had said, and Miranda could not blame him. It was a totally ridiculous explanation. "You will forgive my skepticism, Miss Melbury, if I ask you not to trouble yourself for further explanations. I do not wish to involve you in further flights of imagination."

Miranda had a strong desire to burst into tears. She wanted so much to throw herself on his mercy and explain the real truth. But would he believe her? Anyway, such a course of conduct was out of the question. The earl must consider her the vilest creature in creation, but even that was better than landing poor Aunt Dorothy in trouble. She stood there silently, fighting back the tears which nevertheless began to steal their way down her cheeks.

The earl cleared his throat. "I will drive you home, Miss Melbury," he said in his drawl.

"I have the town coach waiting round the corner for me," sniffed Miranda.

"I will drive you home," he said. "The coach can make its own way back. Come, do not refuse my offer. For Lady Eversley's sake, I would see you back safely. What you do after that is up to yourself."

Miranda felt she could not argue. "Helmslow, my groom, is in the coach. He has my cloak. I would prefer ... prefer not to go home without something to cover up these clothes."

He said nothing but rang for the butler. When that worthy appeared, he commanded: "There is Lady Eversley's coach round the corner. It brought this young person to see me at Lady Eversley's request. You will find that the groom inside it has a cloak. Bring it here, and tell the coachman that I will drive back its passenger."

"Tell the groom that I am quite all right," put in Miranda quickly.

Fields remained impassive, even at the unusual sight of a young whippersnapper interrupting the earl. About five minutes went by, during which neither of the two people in the room spoke. Miranda felt it was the longest five minutes of her life. Then Fields returned with the cloak.

Miranda clutched its ample folds round her thankfully. She felt embarrassed, as never before, in her boy's garb. At home she had felt quite as ease in it, but somehow those days had gone. Somehow she realized for the first time just how shocking an appearance she must present to anyone who knew her true sex. She could not help going red with shame.

Silently the earl accompanied her out of the front door, handing her up to his waiting curricle with what she considered a mockery of courtesy. No words were spoken as the vehicle set off.

As they left the house behind, and were negotiating

the press of traffic at Hyde Park corner, Miranda said in a tiny voice, "I am truly sorry."

"This is not a suitable time to discuss things," said the earl.

Miranda realized that he was warning her not to talk while she could be overheard by the servant perched on the seat at the back of the curricle. But although she understood the need for discretion, his words stung all the same. The silence of that journey back through the height of the daytime press of horse-drawn vehicles and pedestrians was, she thought, almost more than she could bear.

Only once did she venture another remark. It was when, as the earl turned down Knightsbridge at a spanking pace, a small child ran into the road. Without checking, the earl reined the horses to the right, swerving brilliantly to avoid the urchin, then swerving back again at the same reckless pace to avoid a coach that was lumbering in the opposite direction.

Miranda forgot for a moment everything else, and clapped her hands. "Bravo," she could not help saying.

"I do not need your congratulations, Miss Melbury," was the earl's dry reply. And silence reigned until he pulled up at 100 Eaton Square. "I shall not come in with you," he said. "You can count on my discretion." Then without a second look in her direction, he let the horses have their heads and the curricle set off at a spanking pace.

Slowly Miranda climbed the steps and rang the bell. The butler admitted. She was glad she had her cloak around her, when she met his gaze.

"What on earth has happened?" said her aunt, who had been waiting for her return.

"Nothing happened, dear Aunt," said Miranda dully. "We have been mistaken, that is all. It is not the earl who is the blackmailer, but he recognized me, and I have had to make a perfect fandango of nonsense to explain why I should be wearing this disguise."

"Oh, I am so glad it is not the earl," said her aunt, ignoring the rest of Miranda's remarks. "I never did think it could be him. I was so friendly with his dear mother, when I was a young girl." She paused as a thought struck her. "But, Miranda, if it isn't the earl, who on earth is it?"

6

Miranda came to her senses first. "I think this conversation would be best continued in the drawing room, Aunt," she said warningly. Stratton, who had opened the door to her, was as impassive as ever. She glanced at his haughty face. It was the wooden mask of a servant whose ears and eyes were entirely uninterested in what was going on around him. Had he heard? If so, had he understood?

Lady Eversley was blissfully unconscious of Stratton's presence. For a moment Miranda feared that she was going to insist upon immediate enlightenment. To make sure that this did not happen, Miranda turned to Stratton and said, "We have a confidential matter to discuss, Stratton. Could you see that we are not disturbed?"

"Of course, miss," said Stratton with the well-bred butler's bow. Well, he thought privately, something was up, that was for sure. As Lady Eversley's most trusted servant he was well aware that his mistress was in some kind of trouble. Probably the bills, he concluded. He only hoped that the household were not in for one of her fits of economy. It had been Stratton's job to soothe the emotional Alphonse in the kitchens only a year ago, when Lady Eversley had been unwise enough to suggest that he should cut down on the quantities of butter used in the cooking.

With elegant grace, Stratton opened the drawing room door for the two ladies. He was too exclusive a servant to hang round the doorway in hope of overhearing what went on. With stately dignity he made his way back to the downstairs region, to harry the parlormaids and scold the footmen.

Inside the drawing room, Miranda insisted that her aunt sit down on the settee. She fussed round her, offering smelling salts.

"Just tell me, Miranda," wailed Lady Eversley. "I do not want those odious salts. All I want is to know who is the blackmailer, if it isn't the earl."

"That's the trouble, Aunt Dorothy," Miranda said reluctantly. "I still don't know. I have probably exposed myself to total social ruin, and what is worse, I have gained nothing from it. If only I had not thought of the earl . . ." With hasty but carefully chosen words, she told her aunt the full details of that embarrassing encounter in the earl's house.

"So you see, he thinks it was some kind of vulgar prank. He treated me like a silly girl still in the schoolroom. What shall I do when I next meet him?"

"Ten to one you won't meet him again," said her aunt unfelicitously. "He will probably not come near either of us for weeks, if not months. The earl is a dab hand at cutting people. He simply ignores those of whom he does not approve. What a horrid thought." She shuddered.

"But do you think he will tell everybody?" asked Miranda fearfully.

"No. Of course not, child," said her aunt, absentmindedly taking the formerly despised smelling salts from Miranda's grasp. She took a strong sniff of them, making her eyes water. "How odious these are," she gasped. "I had forgot. I can never abide salts. Why did you give them to me?"

Miranda ignored the unjustified reproaches. "If the earl does tell, then both of us are entirely ruined," she said, not without a trace of hope in her voice. "Perhaps I ought to go back to Melbury Place before that happens. And if you came with me, perhaps the blackmailer would not pursue us there."

"Nothing would induce me to set foot in the country during the London season," said her aunt firmly, taking a new and vigorous lease on life. "Really, Miranda, you are too eccentric for words. Of course, Templecombe will not say anything. He may be too fashionable for his own good, but he is nothing if not a gentleman. He will keep his word."

"He may be a gentleman, but I think he is detestable in the extreme," said Miranda with passion.

Lady Eversley gave her a sharp look, drew in her breath as if she was going to say something, then stopped as if she had thought better of it. After a short pause, she said mildly, "Well, this is all quite by the way, Miranda. We still are no further than we were. Poor Mr. Martock," she added inconsequentially. "He will be so upset if the blackmailer tells him."

Miranda swallowed, tried to think, and managed nothing but a blank feeling of dismay. Then suddenly a thought swept into her mind. "Aunt Dorothy," she said, "what about Miss Brassey? You mentioned her when I asked if you had any enemies. If it is not the earl, then it must be somebody else. And it is clear from Miss Brassey's manner that she certainly does not care much for you. Or for me," she added feelingly.

"What makes you say that Jennifer Brassey does not

care for you, Miranda?" asked her aunt with curiosity, always ready to be diverted away from the main topic of the conversation.

"She said something to me after that ride in the park," answered Miranda. "It was something about not knowing Sir Samuel's friends very well, and not mixing in fashionable circles. Her meaning was quite clear. She did not approve of me."

"I have never liked Jennifer Brassey," said her aunt decidedly. "And not just because she is a dowd, though, heaven knows, she is. I would be ashamed to dress so badly. And she has no breeding at all. Who knows where the Brasseys sprang from? They say that their family came from somewhere up north, Cumberland or some such place. But I have never known anybody who has known much about them. There is something very suspicious about jumped-up people of their kind."

"If you feel like that, I am surprised you consented to my engagement to Sir Samuel," said Miranda, rather affronted by her aunt's attack on the Brassey family tree.

"Oh, Sir Samuel is different. If ever there was a man with such natural good taste, and such distinguished manners, and so wealthy . . . I could never understand how he brought down that dowdy Jennifer Brassey to keep house for him. It is not as if she can be amiable to live with. She is nothing but a parcel of good works and dowdy behaviour. Why, she even sent me a letter asking for some considerable sum to give to the Society for the Suppression of Vice. Quite unladylike to ask for money, even if Lady Roehampton approves."

"Aunt Dorothy," asked Miranda quietly, "do you still have that letter by any chance? Because if you do, then I think we should examine the handwriting."

For a second Lady Eversley looked blank, then she sprang to her feet in an access of energy, and rushed to an elegant desk in the corner of the room. "Miranda, you are a marvel," she said, opening the top of the desk.

A huge heap of papers, letters, billets doux, and visiting cards promptly fell out and scattered themselves on the carpet round about. Miranda went to her aunt's assistance, and started picking them up, looking through them as she did. Lady Eversley rummaged inside the desk, through an untidy heap, and more papers fluttered to the ground around her.

"Such brains you have, Miranda," chatted Lady Eversley, as she succeeded in untidying the desk even more. "What a good idea. If only I can find the letter. All these bills! You would not believe how much it costs to run a household, my dear. Look at this. A whole six guineas for butcher's meat." She waved a piece of paper in the air. "All eaten by the servants, I am sure. We never seem to see such luxuries on *our* table."

Miranda wanted to giggle. As she picked up the papers, she thought privately of the delicious dishes concocted in the kitchen by the culinary artist, Alphonse. Thank goodness that the excitable Frenchman was not present to hear her aunt's quite unfounded accusations. Lady Eversley kept a lavish and delicate table, so much so that Miranda had marveled at the wonderful dishes available at every meal.

"Here it is!" shrieked Lady Eversley triumphantly, just when Miranda was beginning to give up hope that the letter would ever be found.

The two ladies went back to the sofa, leaving an unsteady heap of papers on the desk for one of the maids to tidy up. With care, Lady Eversley unfolded a small piece of paper. *"Miss Jennifer Brassey presents her compliments and begs for the favor of ten guineas for the Society for the Suppression of Vice,"* it read.

"The writing looks singularly like," said Miranda with excitement, as she took out the blackmailer's letter from her reticule and smoothed it out. Laid side by side with the other, there was similarity between the two. "The paper is alike, too. Look at it, Aunt Dorothy. The same ink, and I swear that the pen is the same too!"

"Indeed it looks so," said Lady Eversley, carefully regarding the two letters through her lorgnette. "Who would have thought that Jennifer Brassey would have done such a wicked thing?"

"And so careless, too," said Miranda wonderingly. "The woman must be mad. I will take the two letters." Carefully refolding them, she added, "Look, Aunt Dorothy, from the outside they look almost the same. The inscription is the same. That gives me an idea . . ."

She jumped up from the sofa and went toward the door. Then she stopped and thought. "I can't go like this," she said, looking down at the cloak which was still wrapped round her, covering up the boy's clothing beneath.

"Where are you going?" asked Lady Eversley with alarm.

"Why, I am going to confront Miss Brassey and make her confess. What else?" said Miranda firmly.

"You can't go like that," wailed Lady Eversley. "Those terrible breeches! For the love of heaven, Miranda, I beg of you on my bended knees to change your clothes. Jennifer Brassey is a shocking dowd, but she swill have a fit if she sees you so disgracefully dressed."

"I don't care if she has a thousand fits," said Miranda grandly, suppressing a desire to giggle at her aunt's sense of priorities. It occurred to her, though obviously not to Lady Eversley, that shocking Jennifer Brassey would really not matter much. However, she supposed she must be good. "You are right, Aunt Dorothy. I must not be seen like this. After all, I *am* going to Sir Samuel's house, and I would rather die than let him see me like this."

At the thought her face flushed, and she felt hot with shame. She had a lowering feeling that somehow Sir Samuel might find her unconventional garb exciting. She did not wish that. The Beau had a gift for making her feel self-conscious and somehow frightened.

"Are you going to tell *him*?" asked her aunt. "Oh Miranda, should you act so hastily? Shouldn't we try to think this thing through? Besides, it is late and Mr. Martock is taking us to the theater. Have you forgot? 'Twill be most rude not to be there. And what if Miss Brassey denies all knowledge of the blackmail? What shall you do then?"

"I have a plan. Never fear," said Miranda confidently. "I have not made up my mind whether to tell Sir Samuel. After all, if we have the blackmailer then perhaps I shall want to jilt him. If I tell him of his cousin's wickedness, will that not make him more determined upon marriage? I shall see what Miss Brassey's reaction is, when I confront her. Do not *worry*, Aunt. I know what I am doing. I have a marvelous scheme for tricking her into admitting all."

Then when Lady Eversley still looked doubtful, Miranda added: "I shall not do it now. I shall come to the theater with you tonight, and then tomorrow I shall see Miss Brassey. So all you have to do, dear Aunt, is to put all thoughts of the matter out of your head and enjoy the evening. There is a vastly amusing farce, I am told."

Obediently Lady Eversley nodded. Privately Miranda determined that she would visit Miss Brassey just as soon as possible the next day.

Her determination, however, was not enough to allow a morning visit. The day started with a succession of duties that could not be denied. There was a fitting appointment for the new dress that she was to wear that evening. Few alterations were needed, but Lady Eversley insisted that these should be done, even though they seemed of little importance to Miranda.

"My dear, _if_ you go to Lady Jersey's ball in anything but a perfect ball gown, I shall consider I have failed as your aunt," said Lady Eversley in a dramatic way.

She also insisted that Miranda should take a final lesson with Monsieur Duval, and so a whole hour was spent in one of the salons, with Lady Eversley at the piano while Miranda circled round the room in the decorous grasp of the French dancing master. It was, thought Miranda, a terrible waste of time.

It was not until early afternoon that she was free to visit Miss Brassey. As she changed her clothes from the simple round-necked muslin she had been wearing in the morning, she mentally reviewed the task ahead. Miss Brassey undoubtedly disliked her aunt, and had also taken a dislike to Miranda. But how odd of her to stoop to blackmail. How odd to go to such extreme lengths for a mere dislike. Indeed, in one sense her hostility had completely misfired. What she had hoped to gain from blackmail was not clear—unless perhaps she was short of money. Sir Samuel, as all the world knew, was grotesquely rich. But Miss Brassey was only a poor relation. Perhaps the Beau was not as generous as he might be.

Obviously his preference for Miranda had not pleased his cousin. But if only the silly old maid had known—it was *her* blackmailing which had driven Miranda into his arms in the first place. How ironic it was, thought Miranda. Miss Brassey had been the cause of Miranda's getting betrothed. If she had known, how cross she would have been.

Miranda reconsidered what she would wear. She wanted to be dressed fine for this interview, out of defiance toward the dowdy Miss Brassey, who disapproved of high fashion. Yet Miss Brassey had given dear Aunt Dorothy hours of worry. Well, she, Miranda, would show the odious old spinster that she was not to be intimidated. She would wear her most exaggerated finery.

Womanlike, she also thought of Sir Samuel. Her ideas about the Beau were in turmoil, but nevertheless she wanted him to see her at her best, should she encounter him. Of course, she was no longer sure if she wanted to marry him. It looked as if she might not need to be betrothed anymore, not if she could persuade Miss Brassey to confess all and promise to amend.

If she did not need to marry Sir Samuel, whom should she marry? Her thoughts whirled in uncertainty. Through the chaos came the unbidden memory of strong lips on hers. Miranda had to give herself a mental shake. "I hate the detestable Earl of Templecombe," she said aloud to her reflection in the mirror.

From the mirror stared back a dark-haired fashionable lady. They would never recognize her in Mebury Place, thought Miranda. She sighed.

She had chosen one of her most sophisticated walking dresses, of a kind lately featured in *La Belle Assemblée*. A high, ruched bodice in cherry pink silk, was gathered into two ruffles, one high at the neck, the other a little lower across the bodice. At the bottom of the hem were a further two ruffles. Ruffles at the end of its long sleeves peeked out of a cherry-colored pelisse that Miranda wore over the dress. Cherry-colored half boots and a matched parasol showed off her beauty.

To complete the whole, she placed an audacious little bonnet over her dusky raven locks. Its high poke straw was adorned with ribbons and had a cluster of artificial cherries on one side. "Isn't it too elaborate, Aunt Dorothy?" Miranda had asked Lady Eversley when this expensive creation had been first shown to her.

"It *is* elaborate, my child," admitted Lady Eversley, "and certainly not a bonnet that could be worn by anybody. Few girls have the coloring or the air for this kind of bonnet. But on you it looks excessively good."

It was with a certain amount of confidence, therefore, that Miranda made her way down the stairs. Lady Eversley hovered in the hall to see her go. "I have ordered John, the coachman, to wait outside with the carriage," she said anxiously. "Oh no, Miranda, you can't."

"Can't what?" said Miranda, bewildered, awaiting some alarming change of plan.

"Those white gloves," said her aunt firmly. "They spoil the whole look. Wait. Dunn," she ordered, "fetch Miss Miranda the right gloves for this dress. No, Miranda, don't be impatient. It simply won't do to wear white gloves with cherry color. Believe me, I know."

Miranda wanted to giggle again. Here she was setting off to beard a blackmailer in her den, and all her aunt could worry about was getting the right gloves. Lady Eversley really was amazing. She just lived for what was fashionable, and almost her whole mind was entirely taken up with clothes and other frivolities. But it was no use saying anything. Her aunt would simply be hurt and not understand.

Miranda waited patiently till the gloves arrived. They were matching cherry colored. Then she drew them on, rearranged her reticule (which was, fortunately, also cherry colored), and set out.

"That's so much better," called Lady Eversley behind her. "Those white gloves gave you a very off appearance."

Outside the imposing front door of the Brassey dwelling in Park Lane, Miranda's confidence began to ebb somewhat. Back in her aunt's house, it had seemed such a simple thing to do. Now she wondered if she had not overreached herself. What if Miss Brassey simply showed her out? Or refused to listen to her?

Her feelings of fear were at their height as she was shown into an elegant library. All round the room were shelves, reaching from the carpet right up to the ceiling. Large windows, between the shelves, brought the afternoon sunlight into the room. The books were all shapes and sizes, but had all been bound in special green leather. Miranda could not help noticing that the titles were in gold, and there seemed to be a pattern below them. Obviously Sir Samuel had spared no expense. Rebinding every book in a special livery must cost hundreds of pounds, thought Miranda.

There at a small writing desk, with a pair of gold-rimmed spectacles on her nose, looking as disapproving as ever, was Miss Jennifer Brassey. As Miranda entered the room, she put down her pen with a deliberate sigh, and shuffled the papers on the desk. Then deliberately she took her spectacles off her nose. As she stood up, it was plain that she considered this visit an intrusion into her important business. "In what way can I help you, Miss Melbury?" she said in icy tones. "This is a surprise visit. If it is my cousin, Sir Samuel, whom you have hoped to see, then I am afraid he is out at his club."

Her attitude brought all Miranda's rebellious instincts to the fore. She would not be patronized by an old maid in a dowdy gray dress, without an inch of frill. Why, she thought, Miss Brassey was wearing a cap that made her look positively antediluvian.

"I have come on important and confidential business, Miss Brassey," she said formally. "I need to take up some of your valuable time, I am afraid. May I sit down?"

Without waiting for consent, she placed herself in one of a pair of leather-covered armchairs that fronted a coal fire. Carefully arranging her pelisse, she placed her reticule on the arm of the chair and waited for Miss Brassey to sit down too. It was not polite thus to take the initiative, Miranda knew. But she was determined that the acidulous spinster should not get the better of her.

With another angry sigh, Miss Brassey sat down in the other armchair. "I am, of course, delighted to be of help, Miss Melbury," she said in tones that conveyed the exact opposite of delight. "But I am very busy at the moment collecting money for my favorite charity, the Society for the Suppression of Vice. Perhaps you could be brief."

It was an opening that Miranda had been waiting for. "It was about the Society that I came, Miss Brassey," she said, reaching for her reticule. "My aunt asked me whether this letter could possibly have come from you. There was no signature."

So saying, she took out of her reticule a folded piece

of paper. In unmistakable handwriting, it had Lady Eversley's name and direction upon it. She passed it to Miss Brassey, without unfolding it.

Miss Brassey took the folded letter and looked at it. "Yes," she said, "this is my letter to your aunt. I felt sure she would agree with me that the Society is an excellent charity. But I thought I had signed it."

Miss Brassey pursed her lips and screwed up her eyes, as if to convey her disapproval of Lady Eversley. She began unfolding the letter. Then as she glanced at its contents, her faced turned a sickly white. Her fingers trembled furiously, and she dropped the paper on the carpet as if it had been red hot.

Miranda leaned forward from her chair, and seized the paper as it fell. It was the blackmailing letter. Her ruse had succeeded. Miss Brassey had unconsciously revealed that it was her own handwriting, under the mistaken impression that Miranda had handed her the other letter, the letter which had earlier asked Lady Eversley for a donation.

"Now, Miss Brassey," said Miranda fiercely. She got up from the chair and stood over the cowed woman. "I am sure you will agree that you have some explaining to do."

Miss Brassey looked up at her, her faded eyes glowing with emotion. Miranda could not be sure whether they contained hatred or tears. The spinster opened her mouth, as if she would say something, then shut it again. Then with a little half-choked cry, she fell back into the chair.

Miss Jennifer Brassey had fainted.

Miranda was entirely taken aback. This was not at all what she had expected. She looked round frantically for smelling salts but could see none. Feathers . . . that was what she had need of. Burned feathers were the thing . . . But there were no feathers handy either. Miss Brassey was lying back with her mouth open and her eyes shut. A horrid snoring noise came from her lips. Miranda was frightened. She must make her recover.

Desperately she looked round for some kind of help. Then an idea came to her. A couple of strides took her over to the desk, where she seized a piece of thick paper. Perhaps this would burn . . . Stooping to the fire, she lit the corner of it and waved the growing flame under Miss Brassey's nose. She saw the eyelids flicker for a moment, and thankfully snuffed out the flame, placing the piece of paper near her reticule in case it should be needed a second time.

"Miss Brassey, you have fainted," she said sternly to the prostrate figure. "Are you regaining your senses? Shall I call the servants?"

"No, please . . . do not make a fuss. My salts . . . they are in the top-hand drawer in the desk . . . please."

In the desk Miranda found the small jar of smelling salts. Opening it, she waved them firmly under the maiden lady's nose. With a choking sound, and something suspiciously like a sneeze, Miss Brassey opened her eyes and sat bolt upright.

"Oh dear," were her first words. Miranda, to her great surprise, found herself pitying the figure she made. With her cap askew, her short-sighted faded eyes blinking, and her color as white as a sheet, Jennifer Brassey was not a pretty sight.

As soon as she seemed to have gathered her scattered wits somewhat, Miranda started to question her. "You know what that letter contained? A threat to blackmail my aunt. How can you explain it?"

Miss Brassey seemed still dazed. To Miranda's questions she returned no answers, but instead tears gathered at her eyes. They coursed down her cheeks, reddening her eyes and nose. To some women it is given to weep with beauty. But Jennifer Brassey was not one of these.

Miranda began to feel helpless. True, she had unmasked the writer of the blackmail letter, but this was not the ruthless villain she had been led to expect. Miss Brassey was a pathetic and somehow degraded sight. Instead of showing any defiance, or even continuing to demand the money, Miss Brassey showed all the signs of being overwhelmed with misery.

"You understand that we have no intention of paying up or of taking the slightest notice of your outrageous demands?" said Miranda, trying to provoke some kind of reaction.

For the first time Miss Brassey showed signs of life. "It is not what you think, not what you think at all," she sniffed. "I did not ask for that money."

"That is what you wrote in the letter," said Miranda in exasperation. "If it is not blackmail," and she tapped the letter she was holding, "then what on earth were you doing?"

"I am not the blackmailer. It is nothing to do with me." Miss Brassey choked out the words between heavy sobs.

"You wrote the letter? You agree to that much?" Miranda paused. Miss Brassey nodded dumbly. "Then if you wrote the letter," she continued, "why did you ask for money in it?"

"It was nothing to do with me," is all that Miss Brassey would say obstinately. Miranda got the impression that she might have said more, but there was the sound of the front door opening.

Miss Brassey turned even paler, and for a moment

Miranda thought she was going to faint again. "Don't tell him," she whispered desperately to Miranda. "Please, I beg of you. I will do *anything*. Only don't tell him you have found out about my writing the letter. Please, Miss Melbury, by all that is sacred . . . I will explain everything at another time." She was gasping for breath and looked so imploring that Miranda again felt a pang of sympathy.

Footsteps were approaching the door, and it swung open to reveal the immaculately dressed figure of the Beau. With an elegant raising of his eyebrows he surveyed the scene before him.

"Miss Melbury, what a charming surprise!" he said with enthusiasm. "I am so happy, so very honored, that you should visit my poor abode." As he spoke the graceful words, his eyes darted round the room. Miranda thought he missed very little.

She did not quite know why, but she had determined not to tell the Beau about his cousin. She stepped between the two of them so that she shaded the sobbing figure of Miss Brassey from her cousin's keen sight.

"I am delighted to see you, Sir Samuel," she said with equal politeness. "Your cousin is quite overpowered, I am afraid. We were having a delightful little chat, but the heat was too much for her and I am afraid she fainted. I fear I have made her eyes run with too much of the smelling salts. Perhaps you could be so kind as to get her maid to attend her."

He had to respond to such a direct appeal for assistance. As he left the room for a moment to summon the servant, Miranda whispered to the shaken figure of Miss Brassey: "Fear not. I shall not betray you. Not till I have heard what you have to say. Visit us tomorrow. Understand? We must see you tomorrow."

Sir Samuel came back, scowling. "What have you been doing, Jennifer?" he thundered. "I must demand an explanation."

Again Miranda stepped into the breach. "Not now, Sir Samuel," she said imploringly. "Your cousin is ill. Her nerves are shaken. The heat has been too much for her. The smelling salts are too strong, I fear. She needs rest and quiet. She is far too overcome to talk to either of us. You have come in the nick of time to make sure she is taken to her bedchamber."

She talked on desperately, to give Miss Brassey time to recover herself. It seemed to work. By the time an aproned maid came in, Miss Brassey was trying to rise from her chair. She had sniffed back most of the tears, and had succeeded in looking more like a lady who had fainted, than a woman with a guilty secret.

"Thank you, dear Miss Melbury," she managed in a quavering voice, as she leaned on the sturdy arm of the maid. "You have been too kind. I cannot thank you enough. I am sorry about my fainting. Tell Lady Eversley that I will call on you both tomorrow when I am recovered." With a worried look at her cousin, she said nothing more.

"I shall look forward to seeing you," said Miranda with formal politeness. How odd, she thought privately, that I should be actually *helping* her, instead of denouncing her to her cousin. Yet somehow I cannot but feel sorry for her. There is something pathetic about her.

Sir Samuel watched his cousin leave the room with suspicion and ill-temper. Had he been alone with her, Miranda had no doubt but that he would immediately have demanded an explanation. In front of a visitor, he could not. He had to pretend to concern rather than impatience. Even so, his riding whip tapped with impatience against his highly polished boots, as she left the room. And when the door finally closed, he ran the leather thong through the fingers of his left hand, while he looked at the door. Then he turned.

"Now that my cousin has gone off to weep and wail in her bedchamber, perhaps you would be so kind as to tell me what this is all about, Miss Melbury?" said the Beau impatiently.

Miranda could forgive his impatience. It must be tiresome to live with Miss Brassey, she thought. But his words had a jarring note of callousness. "Your cousin fainted. It is not her fault," she said in defense of Miss Brassey. Somehow she did not fancy telling the Beau the truth while he was in this mood.

Perhaps sensing her reluctance and disapproval, he altered his tone. "Divine Miss Melbury, I apologize for my impatience. I rather thought that my cousin may have been vexing you with her talk. No," he held up his hand to halt any words she might be going to utter, "do not deny it. I would not for the world interfere with the goings on among the fair sex. Let us just say that I know my cousin is not enthusiastic about our marriage. Who can blame her? It gives me cause for anger, I have to confess. But her feelings are understandable. She has been mistress of this household for more than a few years. If I marry, it means she must give way to another woman."

"I would not for the world have you believe . . ." started Miranda. She was not sure what she was going to say. Her feelings were in a muddle. What to do, now that she had discovered Miss Brassey's involvement past all doubting? Should she tell all to Sir Samuel? Did she wish to remain betrothed to him? Or would it be best to jilt him? She was much embarrassed, and her sentence trailed off into silence without an ending.

Sir Samuel did not sense her unease. "I assure you, divine Miss Melbury," he continued somewhat pompously, "when you enter this house as my bride, I shall have made my cousin pack her bags. We are not nearly related. It was an act of charity on my part to bring her into the house in the first place. Never fear. I shall pension her off, and she will be quite happy with her tatting and her endless good works in some place like Kensington, out of the fashionable world altogether."

"I would not like her to suffer because of me," murmured Miranda. And, as she said the words, she wondered at them. Somehow she felt no malice toward the wretched and malicious Miss Brassey. Blackmailer she might be, but she was surely the most feeble-hearted of villains!

"You are all generosity," said the Beau smiling. "I shall hope to rival you in generosity of spirit at our wedding. I shall make sure my cousin is well looked after. Only one thing gives me pain."

"What is that?" Miranda was forced to ask. She began to feel nervous about this extended *tête à tête* with no chaperone. Certainly her aunt would not approve of her being alone with a man.

"Only tell me when I may call you mine," said the Beau, still smiling his odd smile. He looked at Miranda with such naked admiration, such naked emotion, that she found herself blushing.

It was not a pleasant blush, nor was it a pleasant feeling that produced it. To cover her confusion, she looked round. "Where is my reticule?" As soon as the words had left her mouth, she realized that it was a mistake to ask. The Beau moved toward her, and from the arm of the chair where she had been sitting he picked up the reticule. By doing so he dislodged various papers. With her heart in her mouth, Miranda realized that he was picking up the blackmail letter.

Fortunately the Beau was far too occupied with her to examined the papers in his hand. He pushed them into the reticule, closed the clasp, and handed it to Miranda. The movement brought him close to her. Too close.

Miranda took the bag, trying to move away without making such a movement obvious. But the Beau took his chance, and snatched at her hands. He drew her, reluctant, toward him. "When am I to have you for my own?" he persisted. "Come, my pretty one, why such blushes?"

With decisiveness, Miranda pulled herself out of his grasp. She was offended by his freedom. His words were those he might have used to a chambermaid, or a trollop of that kind, she thought. "You forget yourself, Sir Samuel," she said tartly. "This talk between us is most improper. I must refer you to my aunt for such questions. The carriage waits outside for me. My aunt was happy to have me wait on your cousin, but I do not think she would condone this interview between us."

"Such prudery, my sweet coquette," said Sir Samuel. There was a hint of irritation in his voice. Then his temper died down and in his usual flowery speech, he went on. "You are even more beautiful when you are angry, my goddess. I will curb my impatience. My time will come soon enough. Do you attend Lady Hatfield's assembly?"

"Yes. Aunt Dorothy says it will be a most agreeable evening. Shall I see you there?" asked Miranda, thankful to have escaped the Beau's importunities. She drew on her gloves ready for departure.

"I shall be there, my fairest. I hope you will honor

me with your delightful conversation, my sweet one, even if you will not grant me further minutes alone," said the Beau. His words were those of the acknowledged lover. Miranda thought he sounded possessive. Too possessive. Her heart sank.

Collecting her dignity together, she nodded graciously and allowed the Beau to escort her to Lady Eversley's carriage, which was waiting outside. The Beau kissed her fingers lingeringly. It was quite correct. But even so Miranda felt uncomfortable. Of course, he was her betrothed—at least until she told him she could not marry him. She could hardly object if he kissed her hand. And yet . . .

"Phew, that was an escape!" She let out a long and most improper whistle of relief as she relaxed against the squab cushions of the carriage, and felt herself driven away from Park Lane. A feeling of great relief came over her.

The encounter with Miss Brassey and the Beau had been trying, most trying. She had so much to tell her aunt. Unconsciously she opened her reticule to check that the blackmail letter was safe. She was slightly taken aback to discover there were three letters there—the blackmail letter, the letter sent by Miss Brassey asking for a charitable donation, and a third one.

Then she remembered seizing the piece of paper to light at the fire to revive Miss Brassey. She must have placed it next to her reticule. Then Sir Samuel had thought it was hers.

For a few minutes good breeding fought with curiosity. Curiosity won. Mentally assigning good breeding to perdition, Miranda unfolded the piece of paper. It was rather burned at one corner, where she had poked it in the fire, but most of the writing could be read.

It was addressed not to Miss Brassey, but to the Beau. The writing was that of an uneducated person. The spelling was vague. The punctuation eccentric. Altogether it was the oddest letter Miranda had ever read. She smoothed out the paper and spread it on her knees, screwing up her eyes so that she could read it in the shadow of the hackney coach. The writing was large and laborious, written by a person whose pen had labored long and uneasily over the formation of the letters

My humble duty to your honor, and hoping you will find satisfaction in what I have done. There is a new shipment of undamaged goods has come to the house, which I have set aside for your honor's inspection.

There is room for them to be sent abroad, shuld you honor see fit to take up the generous offer made by Monsier Brunelle. Or they could be set to work here in the London houses, according to your wishes on the subject.

I await your instructions and orders, your honor. The new girl from the country, whom you wished to see, waits your pleasure. I shall not put her to the work till your honor has said if you have further use for her.

The signature, which was an evil scrawl, was one of a Mistress Madelein Evans.

Miranda read the letter with mystification. It seemed a most extraordinary screed to her. On the one hand there was this mention of goods, and undamaged ones at that, and on the other hand, there was mention of a girl. It seemed possible, she thought, that perhaps the goods were human beings of some kind, but she had never before come across any profession or business where the workers were mentioned in such terms. And yet there was a growing suspicion in the back of her mind, that she hardly liked to recognize. She did not, after all, know much about such goings on. Sir Peter had not sheltered her entirely, as some girls were sheltered. He had mentioned with a laugh that Lord So and So had a woman in keeping, or that the young son of Sir Somebody had ruined the blacksmith's daughter. But these remarks had never meant much to Miranda, or even interested her very much. She had been so much more concerned with horses than humans in her childhood. If she had thought at all about such odd quirks of behavior, it had been only briefly. She had not understood them, and since they did not interest her, had not asked Sir Peter for enlightenment.

The letter she held in her hand frightened her. She knew instinctively that it was something to do with what, in her own mind, she called "love and all that." But whatever it referred to was shameful, dark and horrifying.

Then it occurred to her that perhaps it was something to do with Miss Brassey's exertions on behalf of the Society for the Suppression of Vice. She examined it again carefully. No, it was undoubtedly addressed on the outside to Sir Samuel. Surely if it had been something to do with the Society it would not have been directed to him.

A nameless doubt stirred in the back of her mind. It could not be . . . it was too horrifying. She looked again at the paper. It came from Floral Street, near Convent Garden. By now Miranda had a rough idea of the geography of London and she knew that Convent Garden did not have a very good reputation.

What to do now? Common sense suggested that she should return to her aunt's house. She should tell her of the extraordinary interview, and tell her too of this letter. Miranda studied it again. Yet the letter concerned herself very closely. Miss Brassey might be the blackmailer, but Sir Samuel . . . what should she think of a man who received this letter? Sir Samuel was the man whom she had engaged herself to *marry*.

Perhaps she had misunderstood it. Perhaps it was an entirely innocent letter. Perhaps she would simply be making trouble for Sir Samuel if she showed it to Lady Eversley. She *must* be sure, before she made allegations of this kind, Lady Eversley was so convinced that the Beau was everything that was suave and charming.

In a moment of decision, she signaled to John, the coachman, to stop the carriage. It drew to a halt near a row of hackney carriages.

"John, I have an urgent errand. I cannot explain now. But you will return to Lady Eversley and tell her that I am gone to visit a school friend and that I shall return in an hour."

"How will you go, Miss Melbury?" asked the coachman, touching his forelock. Obviously plucking up his courage, he added: "My lady would not like me to leave you here all alone."

"I shall go by hackney. Now, no arguments, John. Just give my message."

Waiting until the reluctant coachman had driven off, Miranda stood by the line of hackneys. The drivers were smoking pipes and chatting with each other, while their horses stood patiently, some of them dozing in the afternoon sunlight.

One of the drivers was grooming his horse. Miranda thought he looked fatherly, and she approved of his attentions to his beast. She went up to him, ignoring the others, and asked him to drive her to Floral Street.

"Well, Miss, begging your pardon," said the man, straightening himself up from his horse's flanks. "It is not a place I would care to take you to." The well-meaning look on his face robbed the words of any impertinence. "'Tis not that I wish to refuse the fare, I am sure," he added, "but Floral Street is not a place for young ladies like yourself. I don't rightly know if I should be saying this, Miss, but I have two daughters about your age at home, and I should not like to see either of them on Floral Street. Thoses houses there are dens of villainy and no mistake, Miss."

"Well, I shall rely on you to look after me and see that I do not come to harm," she told him. "It is of the utmost importance to me that I go there. I may not need to leave your hackney, but I must have a look at the outside of number eleven."

Obviously thinking he had done his duty by warning her, the driver climbed on the book. Giving his horse an encouraging "Come up, there" they moved off. Miranda noted with approval that he did not so much as touch the horse with his whip.

The drive, itself, was an education. Near Park Lane the houses had been all large and spacious. True, there were mews where stables and coachmen's quarters were huddled together, and where there were heaps of manure and other signs of horses. But on the whole the surroundings were salubrious. Blood horses pulled the carriages in the streets, and even the tradesmen's nags were glossy and well fed.

But as they passed on through the town toward Piccadilly all this began to change. The private houses began to alternate with shops and commercial premises. The main traffic of London, huge, lumbering cart-horses pulling heavy wagons, tiny donkeys with the carts of catsmeat men, and costermongers pulling their own wooden stands, began to take over from the glossy carriages and pairs. There were flower sellers, women with huge baskets of their wares on their heads, tradesmen riding to their business on Welsh cobs, and scores of ragged children that dashed in and out of the traffic regardless of their own safety. The variety and the noise was astonishing.

Nearer Soho, the nature of the shops began to change. Now they were not all of them well painted and smart. Occasionally the hackney went by houses that were frankly dilapidated, peeling with paint, and with broken windows. In small alleyways Miranda could see gangs of ragged young men and women just loafing outside their doorways. The ragged children were now almost all barefoot. The splendid carriages of the gentry got fewer and fewer. Carts and wagons predominated. The very cobbles of the road began to get less well laid, and the smells that rose from them, more offensive. Miranda began to feel rather apprehensive.

The hackney turned into a small lane, where there was barely room for more than one vehicle. Small houses several storeys high overhung the road, most of them with tradesmen's signs in the lower storey. From one of them, a tanner's establishment, came the disgusting smell of the liquids used to cure leather. Miranda sniffed it with horror and remembered how Sir Peter had told her that dog excrement was the principal component. It smelled as if he was right.

The hackney pulled up just past the tanner's. The driver leaned down to her. "The house what you was wanting to see, Miss, is a little way up on the right. 'Tis the one with the yellow paint on the door," he said, keeping his voice low. Already several small boys had turned up to stare at his vehicle and passenger.

"Thank you," said Miranda gratefully. "I think I shall get down and take a walk up the street to see what I can see. I shall be within your view all the time, and so

I do not think anything can happen to me. If it does, then I shall call on you to rescue me." As she spoke, she handed the driver the guinea that Sir Samuel had given her. He pocketed it gratefully and gave her to understand that he would see she was all right.

Getting down from the hackney carriage, she discovered that the streets were far from clean. The vile-smelling liquids from the tannery, and other household wastes too sordid to mention, were running down the middle of the cobbles in a stream. Bits of old cabbage leaves, pieces of old paper, and piles of horse dung were everywhere. Miranda wished she had on a pair of stouter boots.

But nothing daunted, she picked her way down the pavement, keeping her cloak round her. Cautiously she kept to the left side, underneath the overhang of the houses, so as to be out of the way should any housewife decide to add her washing water to the stream flowing down the road. The house she wanted to inspect was on the opposite side.

Slowly she dawdled down the street, looking in the window of a herbalist's establishment, which reflected the bright door of the house opposite. From the outside, there seemed nothing to distinguish number eleven from any other establishment, except its superior quality of paint. But on glancing more carefully, she noticed that the house sported a curious door knocker. It took the form of a classical statue, nothing less than a Venus, clad only in one inadequate piece of cloth. Her heart gave a bound within her when she noticed this. At last she understood what the hackney driver had being trying to tell her. Number eleven was nothing less than a house of ill-fame, a house in which men went in search of abandoned women.

A pang of pure fear rushed through her. She turned, intending to go straight back to the hackney carriage, which was only a few score yards down the street. The driver waved encouragingly to her as he saw her turn back. But from the corner of her eye, she noticed the brightly painted door with its indecent knocker, moving. It opened very slowly and quietly and out stole a young girl. She was gaudily dressed, but what Miranda noticed also was that her face was tear-stained and upset.

For a moment Miranda halted with compassion. But it was none of her business, all the same. She determinedly walked back to the hackney. Just as she was about to climb in, there was the sound of hurried footsteps behind her. Up to the vehicle rushed the same girl. She lifted her tear-stained cheeks to the driver and cried: "Take me, sir. Take me away from here, I beg of you."

"I have a passenger. Can't you see?" said the driver roughly.

With a wild gaze of terror, the girl looked again and seemed to see Miranda for the first time. She fell to her knees, into the muddy filth of the street, regardless of the slime and dirt. "Save me, Miss. I beg of you, save me. Take me with you, for the love of God. They will be after me soon."

Miranda hesitated. "Get in the hackney, then," she said quietly, making up her mind in a flash. She bundled the girl into the carriage, and began to climb in herself.

She halted, as the driver leaned down and said to her: "You shouldn't be doing this, Miss." But just then the door of the house began to open again. "Drive on as fast as you can," said Miranda urgently. The driver, deciding something must be done, whipped up his horse, and the carriage rattled down the street. It passed number eleven so fast that Miranda just caught a glimpse of a huge stout woman with raddled cheeks, and an even larger man who looked rather like a prizefighter. They were standing at the open door looking up and down the street.

She turned to the terrified girl, who was cowering in the corner of the carriage, obviously afraid lest her flight had been detected. "Who are you? And why are you so frightened?" asked Miranda gently.

"Oh Ma'am, thank you. Blessings on you and thank you. They will kill me if they find out where I have gone. Oh what shall I do?" The girl broke into heartbreaking sobs. There was something incongruous about the way she spoke and the clothes that she was wearing. Though the clothes were noticeable for a kind of tawdry finery, her voice was that of a country girl. Its soft burr had not yet been overtaken by a Cockney twang.

"Don't be frightened. You are quite safe with me," said her rescuer. "Where do you want me to set you down?"

At this question, the girl clutched at her protector. Through tears and sobs Miranda could just make out . . . "nowhere to go. Don't desert me."

As the hackney rumbled back through London, Miranda found herself patting the sobbing girl who had given way to her grief and flung her head in Miranda's lap. It became obvious that she could not just turn her out of the hackney. She would have to take her back to Eaton Square. A qualm of dismay struck her. Lady Eversley was the kindest of women and the most hospitable of relatives. She was generous with her charity too. But something told Miranda that she would not take to this girl, who was, alas, far from respectable.

"What's your name?" she asked the sobbing girl.

"Betty Miller," was the muffled response between sobs.

"Where do you come from?"

"From Sussex, Ma'am." The girl seemed to take heart from the fact that she had not been sent down from the carriage. She sat up and made ineffectual attempts to wipe away the tears that were still pouring down her cheeks. "Oh, Ma'am, I've not been long in London. I thought it was a respectable servant's place I was taking . . ."

Again, the violence of her emotions seemed to overpower her, and she broke down again. Miranda gave up all hope of getting a reasonable explanation for her distress. Questions would have to wait for a bit.

At this moment the hackney drew up in front of Lady Eversley's house. "Thank you kindly, Miss," smiled the driver as he pocketed a second coin handed to him by Miranda."

"Thank you, too," said Miranda politely. "You were such a help." She climbed out and helped Betty to get out too. The girl clung to her as if to her last hope, and it was with difficulty that Miranda got her up the steps to the front door.

Stratton opened it, and Miranda almost wanted to laugh as she saw an expression of horrified dismay, followed by wooden lack of feeling, come over his countenance. She went into the hall, still with the hapless girl clutching at her.

"Shall I ask the young person to wait in the kitchens?" suggested Stratton. He had controlled his face so that it wore its usual air of hauteur.

"No, Stratton," said Miranda firmly. "I am taking Betty up to my bedchamber."

Miranda halted, undecided. Then she realized that

time was getting on. If she was to attend Lady Hatfield's assembly, she must get ready. "You go with Stratton," she told the girl. "He will find you something to eat, I daresay, and somewhere to sleep for tonight. I will see you in the morning."

She gave the girl a little push toward Stratton, whose face conveyed his distaste for the task assigned him. The girl looked panic-struck for a moment, then she bobbed a little curtsey to Miranda and turned to go, looking rather like a victim assigned to a fate unknown.

Miranda went upstairs. There was no time to talk to Lady Eversley. It was late. She must get ready. As she dressed, her mind was not entirely on the proceedings, and she found herself impatient with the maid who was brushing her raven hair. Then all her dresses seemed somehow dowdy. She was sure that Diana Hatfield would be wearing more becoming garments. Altogether, she was discontented at the thought of the evening ahead. Sir Samuel would be there, and she would have to pretend she knew nothing but good about him. An even more alarming possibility was that she would be required to face the Earl of Templecombe.

It was an unhappy girl who joined Lady Eversley at the last minute in her carriage. After several changes of mind, Miranda had chosen a dress of pale blue, ornamented with becoming pink ribbons at the bodice, and more ribbons at the flounce round the hem. A blue fillet among her raven curls and long blue matching gloves drew a nod of approval from her aunt, who surveyed her dress before they left.

In the carriage, Miranda felt it her duty to tell her aunt that Miss Brassey's guilt had been plain. "Whoever would have thought it?" was Lady Eversley's reaction. "I never liked her but it surprises me, Miranda, that she is

145

capable of such infamy. I hope her perfidy will not change your feelings toward dear Sir Samuel. He cannot be blamed for his cousin's faults."

Miranda held her tongue with difficulty. She longed to tell her aunt about her discovery of Sir Samuel's odious involvements in a vile trade. But such a revelation might disturb her aunt's composure, and Miranda was very conscious that Sir Samuel would be in attendance this evening. She did not wish *him* to know—yet—about her discovery of Floral Street. She needed time to think what to do.

So just for this one evening it was necessary to mask her feelings and present a smiling face to the Beau. If she told her aunt the truth, she did not think that Lady Eversley would be capable of such deception. Better to tell her the next day. Nor had she revealed the disturbing presence of Betty to her aunt. Miranda knew that there would be opposition from Lady Eversley when she told her that this girl had to be rescued.

Sir Samuel was there, as he had promised. So was the Earl of Templecombe.

There started an evening that could only be described, thought Miranda, as a nightmare. Immediately she and Lady Eversley walked into the house, Sir Samuel came to their side. He showered them with compliments. He ogled Miranda. He flattered her. He clung to her side, and stuck like a burr. He disgusted her.

She could only be grateful that she had not told Lady Eversley about the true nature of this polished man at her side. She did not think her aunt could have borne his presence. She, herself, found it difficult to bear. He was loathsome. Every time he paid her some full-blown compliment, she thought of that sordid house in Floral Street. When he complimented her on her dress, the tawdry finery of Betty came into her mind. When he took her hand to lead her into a dance, it was all she could do not to snatch it back. As she thought of other flesh that he had touched, she felt sick.

He sat by her side, while the lovely blonde Diana Hatfeld entertained some of the company in a side room with music on the piano. She played well, thought Miranda. The Earl of Templecombe obliged the smiling beauty by turning the pages of her music.

Lady Hatfield broke in on her reverie. The pair of them were smiling at some private joke, as Diana took a break from playing. Miranda was gloomily looking at the Earl's evident enjoyment.

"Do you play the piano? Would you be so kind as to oblige us with some music, after Diana has finished?" asked Lady Hatfield.

"I fear I do not play," said Miranda quietly.

"Not play the piano? Your instrument is the harp, perhaps?" persisted Lady Hatfield. "Or perhaps you prefer the violin, Miss Melbury?"

"I do not play any musical instrument. I was not taught," said Miranda baldly.

"How remiss of your parent, Miss Melbury," twittered the lovely Diana's mama. "Music is such a comfort to one. I am sure that Diana finds it so. I believe that every young woman should play, and I made sure she had the best teachers. She is very accomplished as a result. And gentlemen are so fond of music. I am sure that the Earl of Templecombe seems quiet entranced." She smiled archly, quite aware that her comments could give no pleasure to the girl who was her daughter's rival.

"Miss Melbury has other accomplishments," put in Beau Brassey, who was sitting nearby.

Lady Hatfield gave him a malicious look but vouchsafed no reply. After a pause, her daughter began on another piano sonata and the mother drifted off to talk to the other guests.

Miranda felt smirched. That she should need defending by a man like Sir Samuel! The piano playing was interminable. The assembly was tedious. She had a headache and the chatter around her bored her. The earl had only bowed when he saw her, from a distance. There had been none of his distinguishing attentions. He had paid court to Diana Hatfield instead.

Miranda thought that both he and Beau Brassey were odious. It was, she decided, a horrid evening.

7

It had been a horrid evening, too, for Betty, the girl Miranda had rescued.

The bombshell of Betty's presence burst the next morning when Miranda met Miss Dunn, the dresser, who said with an acid smile, "I hope that the young person will not be staying long, Miss Miranda. I am sure that she is not happy here. It's a very bad example, if I may say so, Miss, for the kitchen maids not to mention the youngest housemaid."

"She is in trouble, Dunn," said Miranda, trying to touch the heart of the upper servant. "She needs our help. It is our Christian duty to do our best for her."

"I am sure it is not part of anybody's Christian duty, Miss, to come near a girl who is no better than she should be. If you will forgive me, Miss, she is more like something out of Babylon than out of this country. There is only one answer for girls like that, and it isn't taking them into respectable households where they may corrupt others. And I hope that Lady Eversley will see my point, for I wouldn't be doing my Christian duty unless I told her of the uproar that girl's being here has caused below stairs."

Miranda was startled by the strength of hostile feeling

from Dunn. Her brow furrowed, and she wondered what she could do about it. She had had some vague idea of finding Betty a job in the kitchens but obviously that would not do. Right or wrong, the unrelieved contempt of the other servants would probably mean that the poor girl would run away. And for her, there would be only one way of life to run to.

She sighed, and her mind went back to the extraordinary fact that Betty had revealed. Somehow Sir Samuel was involved with that house of ill fame. The letter proved it. What a very strange muddle it all was. Here was Miss Brassey on the one hand trying to help fallen women, and on the other trying to blackmail her aunt. And then here was her cousin, Sir Samuel, engaged apparently in ruining the same fallen women. . . .

"I am a complete idiot," said Miranda out loud, as she went downstairs. Her spoken remark made one of the housemaids jump, and look up from her task of dusting the fine banisters. "Don't worry, Jane," said Miranda, "I was just talking to myself."

A moment of revelation had suddenly come to her.

Of course, it was obvious. If Sir Samuel were villain enough to have dealings with bawdyhouses, he would certainly not stop at blackmail. The two Brasseys must be in it together.

Letting herself into the drawing room, Miranda sank down on one of the delicate Chippendale sofas. It was time to think this thing out. She cast her mind back to Lady Eversley's original tale of the unhappy poet. She remembered that the romantic Mr. Ambrose had apparently been killed in a street brawl "in a vulgar bit of London." Those had been her aunt's words. Ten to one, thought Miranda, unconsciously lapsing into the talk of the stable, that the brawl had been somewhere near, or even in, the Floral Street house. Probably the madame of the establishment had gone through his pockets to see if there were anything of interest.

Once she had found the letters from Lady Eversley, what better use than to turn them over to Sir Samuel. He would know about high society. Perhaps another source for his wealth was blackmail. Then he in his turn would tell all to his cousin.

At this point Miranda's racing brain halted. What of the pathetic Jennifer Brassey? She remembered the spinster's evident fear of her cousin, her imploring words, begging Miranda's silence. Were those just the result of guilt? Or did they reflect the woman's fear of her cousin's wrath? Just how far in the blackmail plot *was* Miss Brassey?

The whole business began to take on a different complexion. Miss Brassey obviously *had* known, but perhaps she had been merely the unwilling instrument, rather than the eager accomplice, of Sir Samuel? That would make sense of her behavior yesterday.

Miranda heaved a sigh and concentrated furiously. Sir Samuel had been his normal urbane self that evening at Lady Hatfield's assembly. He could not possibly have smiled so long and so enthusiastically had he known that his plot was revealed. Miss Brassey, for some reason or other, must have concealed the real cause of Miranda's visit from him.

Well, this was surely matter for thought. Miranda realized that she must lose no time in making sure that Lady Eversley knew the real state of affairs. It was not an entirely happy thought. While Miranda had felt confident that she could bully Miss Brassey into ceasing her blackmail demands, she had much less confidence in her powers of dealing with Sir Samuel. There was something both sinister and impressive about the man.

Lady Eversley was to be found trying on a new turban. Characteristically, the chair near the mirror was piled high with different bonnets and headdresses. Miss Dunn was standing by, looking extremely bad tempered.

"Miranda," said Lady Eversley in worried tones, "what on earth is all this I hear about fallen women? Dunn is in a terrible state about it, and Stratton too. What is this girl you brought back yesterday, and why did you not tell me about it before we went to the Hatfields'. It is too bad of you. And that reminds me to tell you that it is not at all the thing to go jauntering round London in a hackney cab without a chaperone."

"Sorry, Aunt Dorothy," said Miranda not very penitently. "But it was all too complicated to explain last night. I didn't want to spoil the assembly for you. Besides, there is a lot I must tell you now. Perhaps Dunn would be so good as to leave us together." She spoke with calm firmness, which seemed to impress the fierce upper servant. Merely smiling grimly, she left the room.

"Well, Aunt, when I told you about Miss Brassey, I think I may have been mistaken." Miranda launched into her tale. "I have reason to believe that Sir Samuel is also blackmailing you, and that his cousin may simply be his unwilling tool. What is more he is deep-dyed in all sorts of other villainy. That's where the girl comes in. I rescued her from a house of ill-fame, which I believe is run by a woman on behalf of the Beau."

"Beau Brassey and a house of ill-fame?" Lady Eversley stared into the mirror as if she could see the Beau there. "Dearest Miranda, are you sure? Why, you were smiling at him only last evening. He is your betrothed. Oh dear, what a terrible scandal!"

With only the slightest pause, she continued. "I hardly know what to say, Miranda, but I do know one thing. It is quite out of the question for you to concern yourself with that girl. We have nothing to do with that class of woman. You should not even know such things. Young girls don't. I cannot help but feel that you have been imposed upon by some designing woman. Depend upon, this is some cock-and-bull story from a vulgar chit from the gutter. They tell me that that class of woman is always a liar, though I am happy to say I know little about it. Lord Eversley would never have mentioned such things."

She paused for breath in her rambling denunciation. Miranda managed to slip a few words in, before the monologue continued. "Now, dearest Aunt Dorothy, this is a good girl. I give you my word for that. She is just a country lass who has been shamefully used. Come and see for yourself. I have ordered her to be in my room."

"I wouldn't dream of bandying words with her," said Lady Eversley with alarming firmness. "Nothing would make me so demean myself as to meet a woman like that."

"But Aunt Dorothy, you must. This girl is important. She may be able to help us outwit Sir Samuel. If she can confirm that he is the man who runs her . . . er, her establishment, then we can demand the letters back by threatening *him* with exposure."

"Even so, Miranda, you should not be having anything to do with the girl," said her aunt obstinately, but her tone was weakening, and Miranda thought she noticed a gleam of curiosity in her eyes. "I will lay you odds she is not at all the hard-done-by female you have told me of. She is just a shameless hussy, I have no doubt."

But to Miranda's relief, she stepped back from the mirror, took off the turban, and cast it upon the heap of other bonnets on the chair. Pausing only to pick up a richly embroidered Paisley shawl which she draped negligently round her shoulders, she followed her niece out of the room. True, her expression was one of unrelenting disapproval, but Miranda thought this might soften when she met Betty for herself.

Betty was ordered up from the bowels of the house to Miranda's bedchamber. As she opened the door, she looked extremely nervous and more than a little depressed. She gave a bob curtsey, as country girls do, and stood nervously twisting her handkerchief, her eyes set firmly on the carpet.

In the morning light, Miranda could not help acknowledging that the girl was shockingly dressed. Her high-waisted gown was cut so low as to reveal a great deal of bosom, and the hem was high enough to display a shapely but not entirely clean ankle. The first thing to do would be to get her some respectable clothes, thought Miranda. Dressed as she is, nobody could mistake her profession.

The girl bobbed another curtsey, and for a moment it looked as if she was going to burst into tears. Then Lady Eversley intervened. "Now then, girl," she said in haughty tones, "I want an explanation."

"Please Madam," said Betty, curtseying for the third time in desperation, "I know that I didn't ought rightly to be here, but I was that feared when I left the house that I was desperate. I will go, if it please you."

"No, no, there is no need to go yet," said Lady Eversley more kindly. "I would like to know what you were running away from, and why you decided to leave so quickly. No lying now; my niece leads me to believe that you were in nothing less than a bordello. I want the truth."

"Well, Ma'am, 'tis true. I been there some ten days, I reckon, since I came up to London and I never did get the chance to slip out, but that once. So I took it. They locked me up the first week, then after . . . after the gentleman had had his way, I was let out." Her voice broke, and she burst into sobs. Through her tears she continued her pathetic story. "So after that I didn't rightly know what to do. I couldn't go home, not after what had . . . had been done. My parents is respectable folk, you see. So as I thought I must make the best of it. But somehow I couldn't put my mind to being that kind of thing." Her voice trailed off.

Miranda decided to take a hand in the questioning. "It was a brothel you were kept in?" she asked directly. Lady Eversley shuddered.

The girl looked up from the carpet for the first time and into Miranda's eyes. "It was that," she said, blushing. "I didn't know when they took me there, I swear on the Bible, Ma'am," she continued, turning imploringly to Lady Eversley. "The woman who hired me seemed so nice-spoken, and she said I was to be her maid."

"We believe you, Betty," said Miranda reassuringly. "But how on earth did you get yourself into such a pickle? We would also like you to tell us everything you know about that woman. We must know, child, if we are to help you."

"Well, I comes up to London by wagon to find work, for there was none at home. My Mam told me to be careful, and so I was, but I never thought to find such deception and the snares of the wicked. Why, when I first met Mistress Cole, I thought she were the widow of a tallow maker. And a right kind mistress I thought she would be, and she telling me that she needed a maid, it seemed like Providence was looking after me."

"Where did you meet her?" asked Miranda patiently.

"At the inn where the wagon put me down, Ma'am. I was going to see my cousin in Kensington and stay with her till I found a post, but Mistress Cole comes up just as I get down from the wagon and asks if I wanted to work. I thought it was a great chance and so I says yes promptly."

"Does Mistress Cole . . . er . . . run the house where she took you?" asked Miranda hesitantly, groping for the right words.

"Oh yes, Ma'am. She is over all the girls and is very strict. If you don't give satisfaction, then it is out of the house, only they don't let you go where you choose. You is shipped off somewhere, I don't rightly know where, but to foreign parts, so the other girls tell me. Mistress Cole has Mr. Bruteson to help her. He is an old prizefighter and comes in handy if the gentlemen get too drunk. And then there is the man, the gentleman I should say, who owns the house."

"Who is he? Do you know his name?" asked Miranda, trying to keep the excitement out of her voice. This was the information she needed. Here was the witness who would give her and Lady Eversley a weapon against the odious Beau Brassey.

"I don't know his name, Ma'am," said Betty, "but they calls him the Beau. He is a main fine gentleman, and very rich, they say. He came to the house but once when I was there."

Miranda turned to her aunt. "You see. If we can but contrive for Betty to get a look at Sir Samuel, she may be able to recognize him. I have not told you yet why I think it is he. But this is the letter that made me think he might be involved."

She took the letter that she had picked up from Sir Samuel's desk out of her reticule and handed it to her aunt. Quickly she outlined what had happened during her visit. Lady Eversley nodded as she spoke, almost dazed by the information. She read the letter slowly.

"Did you ever meet a lady with the fine gentleman, Betty?" Miranda asked the girl, while her aunt pored over the letter.

"No, Miss," said Betty. "There was only Mistress Cole, but I know that she is no lady, not a real lady, you might say. Otherwise it was just the girls like me."

"It looks as if you are right about Beau Brassey," said her aunt, having read through the letter. She handed it back to her niece. "What a terrible scandal. Who would have thought it? Sir Samuel has been so much feted. Why, even Lady Jersey has been close to him. It will be a terrible shock for her. Half the hostesses in London will have cause to blush when this is discovered."

"I do not think it is necessary that we should discover it at all," said Miranda thoughtfully. She had pondered what the best tactics would be. "You see, Aunt Dorothy, all we want is the return of your letters. It is not in our interests to reveal the truth about the Brasseys. Were we to do that, Sir Samuel might simply publish the letters. Better by far to use this information simply to get our letters back, and put an end to the blackmail."

"But do you not think we owe a duty to society," said Lady Eversley doubtfully "Think, Miranda, the man may be blackmailing others. I think we should make a push to expose him for what he is Besides, how on earth can I go on meeting him. I can hardly cut him altogether without some explanation, and I do not know how I should manage if I were forced to talk to him."

As she spoke, there was the sound of a carriage

drawing up at the house. Miranda ran over to the window and looked out. It was a phaeton, with two bays, driven by Sir Samuel. "You may be forced to talk to him sooner than you think, Aunt," said Miranda. "Quick, Betty, come to the window and take a look. Is that the man you saw in the house?"

Betty came over to the window. With a little cry she shrank back, covering her face with her hands. "Oh 'tis him, Ma'am. 'Tis he come to bring me back. Oh Ma'am please save me," she fell to her knees, clutching at Miranda's skirts, looking up pitifully. "I'll do anything, Ma'am, but don't give me back. I'd kill me'self rather than live that life of shame again."

Miranda looked at the girl, then to her aunt. She thought quickly. "Aunt Dorothy, you will have to go and entertain him until I come down. I must put on something more fit to receive him, and deal with Betty here. Remember, he does not know that *we* know about him. He does not even know that we know he is the blackmailer."

"I can't" wailed Lady Eversley in an alarmed flutter. "What shall I say to him. Besides, I am in undress."

"You must. Just do the polite thing, Aunt Dorothy. I shall come down in a little while. Then you may leave us together. I will deal with Sir Samuel, don't you fear. Remember now," she added as her aunt turned to go, "don't let him suspect anything for the moment."

She turned back to the girl who was still kneeling and weeping at her feet. "Now, Betty," she said, "Get up and be a good girl. I am not going to hand you over to Sir Samuel. You are quite safe here. Only you cannot stay here in London."

"Oh, no, Ma'am. 'Twould not be safe," said the frightened girl getting to her feet.

"Well, I have been thinking, and I shall send you

down to where I live in the country, Betty. My old nurse lives there, and I will ask her to find you a job. Would you like that?"

"Oh yes, Ma'am," breathed the grateful girl, her eyes shining.

"But you must promise me to be a good girl from now on," said Miranda. "We shall not tell anybody about your life in London. You must put that right out of your mind, and forget that it ever happened. From now onward, you must lead a quiet life. I shall find you some respectable clothes before you go. The ones you have on would never do."

"Thank you, Ma'am. I shall be good. 'Twas all I ever wanted, to have a good post and live quiet and decent," said the girl, bobbing a curtsey. "And now can I help you with your dress, Ma'am."

"Yes, Betty, you may," said Miranda graciously. "I think I shall change into my blue cambric." It was a round frock with muslin flounces, richly embroidered in Clarence blue. A silk Spencer of the same color, with wide cuffs of white satin, and a Castillian fichu with a full Spanish ruff completed the dress. Miranda picked up a pair of yellow Limerick gloves, and a light fringed Cashmere shawl in pale blue.

She felt the need to dress up, if only to give herself courage to deal with Sir Samuel. It was therefore with an air of unapproachable dignity that she entered the morning room.

She found Lady Eversley chattering nineteen to the dozen to a rather bored Sir Samuel. Obviously Aunt Dorothy had been frightened that she might not manage the conversation and so she had gone to an extreme of talk. She was telling Sir Samuel about Lady Jersey's ball that evening, describing the dress she would wear, mentioning the inclement weather they were having this summer, and scarcely allowing the Beau to get a word in edgeways.

Faced with this flow of small talk, Miranda had to admit that Sir Samuel's manners were impeccable. He smiled, and looked as if he was deeply interested.

"Good afternoon, Sir Samuel," said Miranda with a dignified nod in his direction. Her aunt looked relieved at her entrance. Sir Samuel came across the room, and gave a low bow, kissing her hand in what Miranda could not help feeling was a proprietory manner. "Aunt Dorothy," Miranda said, "Dunn wants a word with you."

Lady Eversley picked up her cue. "I hope you will forgive me, Sir Samuel," she said immediately. "I must go and see Dunn." She bustled out of the room rapidly.'

Miranda turned to Sir Samuel. "It was a pretext, sir," she said, "to get my aunt out of the room. I have something I must say to you alone."

"I am flattered, dear goddess. What counts convention?" Sir Samuel moved toward Miranda, as if he was going to take her in his arms. With a quick movement she countered by sitting down upon one of the little gilt chairs. The Beau was forced to sit on one near her.

"Sir Samuel, I cannot marry you," said Miranda getting straight to the point. "And what is more, I have something excessively unpleasant to tell you. I know about number eleven, Floral Street."

A look of fury drifted across the Beau's face. Miranda thought he was going to be violent, but he got control of himself. Only his knuckles, gripping the arms of the chair, were white with tension. He gave a harsh laugh. "So, my beauty. Surely you do not shock that easily. Or are you hurt that my attention has strayed to other women? I assure you my interest in them is only one of business. For all I care, their charms might be at the bottom of the sea. Only they are exceedingly profitable."

With difficulty Miranda kept her temper. "You are making money out of human misery and human vice," she told the Beau. "I could not marry a man whose fortune proceeded from such a sordid source." She stood up.

It was an unwise move. The Beau stood too, and moved swiftly. Before she could evade him, he pulled her into his arms. His face hovered threateningly close to hers.

Miranda froze. Then in a quiet voice, she went on: "I also know that you and your cousin have been blackmailing my aunt."

The Beau dropped his arms immediately and took a step backward in amazement.

"I want those letters back, Sir Samuel," said Miranda in the same quiet tones. "I think you will return them. You see, if you do not, then I shall tell the world that Sir Samuel is a trader in young girls. That will look shocking, will it not? Especially since your cousin has been so prominent in the Society for the Suppression of Vice." Then, in answer to a gesture on his part, she added: "I have proof. I have the letter written by Mistress Cole, addressed to you, and what is more I have a witness from that house who can swear to having seen you there."

"What an efficient young lady you are, my dear," said Sir Samuel, striving for coolness. "And what an inexpressively inefficient silly old maid I have for a cousin. I should have guessed when I walked in. Fool that I am. I thought there had been some maidenly spitefulness, no more."

He paused for thought, and an expression of wonder came over his face. "You cunning little minx. I'll lay odds you persuaded that goose of a woman to confess all. I see I have underestimated you, Miss Melbury. I suppose you stole my correspondence under her very eyes. Or did you persuade her to hand it over?"

There was a menacing tone his his voice which boded ill for the pathetic Miss Brassey. "She did not hand over anything, Sir Samuel," said Miranda. "Nor did she admit anything, except that she had written the blackmail letter. She could hardly deny it. The writing was so similar to a letter she had written asking for a donation. Besides, I tricked her."

"That damned busybodying Society," swore Sir Samuel. "I told her to give up her do-gooding schemes, but she would not heed me. Well," he said, recovering his temper. "There is no more to be said about the letters. You will have them back, as soon as I return home. I will send my valet round with them, if you will be so kind as to give him the letter you have. I cannot think how you gained possession of it . . ."

Miranda did not think she need enlighten him that it was the merest chance she had picked up that paper, rather than some other, in her search for something to burn to bring back Miss Brassey's senses. Let him think he had been outwitted by some daring plan. It was so much the better.

Sir Samuel was still staring at her, as if trying to work out how such a slip of a girl could have outwitted him. Then he said seriously: "You and I would make a wonderful couple, my dear. You have not only spirit but wit, too. With my skill for business, and your beauty and intelligence, there is nothing we might not achieve. Think about it. I want you more than ever."

"You must be mad," said Miranda disdainfully. "I

would not stoop so low as to join my fate to a man who makes a living out of a sordid and shameful traffic."

"Does it make you jealous, sweetheart?" asked the Beau, apparently in all seriousness. "Think no more of it. Those girls are no more to me than so much cattle. I have never mixed business with pleasure. Does that surprise you? I love you for yourself, you know."

"It doesn't surprise me because I don't believe it," said Miranda tartly. "I have a pretty good fortune that would come in useful now that you will have to give up some of your more sordid money-making schemes."

The Beau laughed "It is you I want, not your money. Let us say that your fortune at first attracted me, as much as your beauty. But now I should like to wed you for your own fair sake. Never before has any woman worsted me. You have come off with the honors, it seems. And I would give anything, believe me, anything, to have you for my own."

He sounded entirely as if he meant it. His very sincerity frightened Miranda. "Well, you can't marry me," she said childishly. "Our engagement is at an end."

"We shall see," was all that the Beau said. He looked round for his silver-topped cane which he had left standing against the chair. "We shall see," he repeated, looking at Miranda through his quizzing glass.

"I do not think there is anything further to say," said Miranda. She went over the mantelpiece and rang the bell. "Show Sir Samuel out," she said to Stratton.

The Beau paused by the door, and looking back intensely at her, said mockingly, "I hope I shall have the pleasure of seeing you at Lady Jersey's ball tonight."

"All I want from you, Sir Samuel, is the letters you have promised," said Miranda snappishly.

"Your wish is my command, my beauty," said Sir Samuel, giving an elegant parting bow. With a slight smile on his lips he left the room. As the front door closed, Miranda went to the window to make sure that he was going. As he got into his phaeton, he kissed his fingers at the window, as though he knew that she would be there. She drew back crossly.

Lady Eversley came bustling back into the room. "Miranda, how did it go? Have you got the letters?" she asked.

"Not yet. But he promised to send them round as soon as he reaches his home. In return I am to give him the letter I stole from his desk," said Miranda almost absentmindedly. She was thinking worriedly about Betty. "You know, Aunt Dorothy, Sir Samuel is much more sinister than I thought. I think we should send Betty away as soon as possible."

"Oh, I agree," said Lady Eversley with worldly relief. "Give her some money and let the girl be on her way. It is not suitable for her to stay here."

"No," said Miranda firmly. "I have got to look after her. I am sending her down to Melbury Place, where she can live quietly and nobody need know her shameful past. I will ask Helsmlow to take her down tomorrow. I am afraid Sir Samuel will find some means of harming her if she stays here."

Just then there was a knock at the door, and Stratton appeared, clearing his throat. "Sir Samuel's valet is here, Miss Melbury," he said portentously. "It appears he has a package for you, but he insists on handing it over to you personally. He says that you have something for him in exchange. I have put him in the library."

"Send him in, Stratton," said Miranda. She drew the

letter from her bosom. She had kept it there during her interview with the Beau in case he disputed its existence. As the valet came into the room, she held it out to him. "You have something for me in return, I think," she said.

"Yes, Miss," said the valet, not altogether respectfully. He too held out a package, but kept a firm grip upon it until Miranda put her letter in his other hand. "My master sends his greetings, and begs you to reconsider his offer," he said.

Miranda said nothing. She pounced on the package and opened it, counting the letters. "Are they all there," she asked her aunt.

"Thank goodness, yes, they are," said Lady Eversley, clutching at the somewhat grimy sheets of paper.

"Thank you," said Miranda, nodding to the valet. The servant left the room.

"Oh, Miranda, how can I ever thank you enough?" Lady Eversley fell upon her niece in a flurry of *Eau de Venus,* clasping her to her bosom. "My dearest child, this is all your work. But I am afraid it is a sad business, losing Sir Samuel like that. Not that he could have made a good husband, but who would have thought that he would turn out to be such a shocking villain?"

"I don't care two straws about losing *him,*" said Miranda stoutly. "I only got engaged to him because I thought it might be a way of getting some money out of Mr. Scrimgeour. You mustn't worry about me, dearest Aunt. Just you marry your Mr. Martock and be happy. I shall go alone very happily, don't you doubt. There will be other offers."

Even as she said the brave words, she felt rather glum. Somehow none of the gentlemen who might offer for her seemed at all attractive. Except the earl, of course, and he was not likely to look at her again. "The Earl of Templecombe will be at Lady Jersey's tonight," she said, trying to make her voice casual.

It did not deceive her aunt. "Oh Miranda," sighed Lady Eversley, "don't say that you too have fallen victim to his charms. The earl has broken more hearts than any man I know. Not that I am surprised, my pet. For I am sure he singled you out in a very promising way at your come-out. But I fear he did the same last night for Lady Diana. We must not hope for more distinguished attentions. Besides, after he found you in boy's clothing, what must he think? The Templecombe family is a stickler for good behavior, I fear."

"I suppose you must be right, Aunt," said Miranda listlessly. "It would be foolish of me to expect the great Lord Templecombe to take any more notice of me. I daresay he only distinguished me with his attentions in the first place to oblige you."

"Well," said her aunt in a voice designed to cheer her niece, "I can only say that if you wear the dress Madame Latour made for you, I daresay you will be swamped by admirers, even if Templecombe isn't among them."

Miranda's spirits lifted. It was impossible to be gloomy with a ball of such magnificence ahead. She knew, too, that her ball gown would be as beautiful as any there. "I shall not look a mean thing," she said aloud.

"I should think not. You will look the most beautiful of the young girls there," said her aunt loyally. "And I shall be most surprised if you don't make as big a hit tonight, as you did at your come-out. It is said that the prince regent will be there. He asked Templecombe a week ago if he would be attending, and when Templecombe said that he would, the prince said he would be there too. It is wonderful how he depends on the earl's advice, now that poor Beau Brummell is abroad."

"Oh, bother the earl," said Miranda crossly and ran from the room.

8

The scene in Lady Jersey's ballroom was one of breathtaking magnificence. Everywhere Miranda looked she saw rich jewels, fine silks, diaphanous muslins, rich embroidery, and handsome men and women. All the beauty and elegance of high society were there, crowding into the supper room, chattering in corners, elegantly going through the steps of the cotillion on the dance floor.

Miranda and her aunt had arrived a little late, escorted as usual by the faithful Mr. Martock. Miranda looked happily toward a corner of the ballroom where her aunt was seated. Mr. Martock was in close attendance. From the look in his eyes, and the ardent fashion in which he anticipated all her aunt's wishes, it would not be long before he proposed. Dear Aunt Dorothy deserved some happiness, and he was a man who would look after her, cherish and protect her, thought Miranda.

There was no doubt that this was the ball of the season. On their arrival the square had been a flurry of carriages, link boys holding flaming torches, and footmen helping the carriages' dazzling occupants to descend. Miranda had never before been to so large a function.

She was looking very beautiful. For this grandest of

all occasions, Lady Eversley had dressed her charge in a deceptively simple white muslin ball gown, very much a young girl's gown. It was beautifully cut to outline her slender young body, its langorous curves, and the high, pointed breasts. Only the simplest of embroidered forget-me-nots decorated the hem, the bodice, and the tiny puffed sleeves. Otherwise Miranda's toilet was very very simple. White satin slippers and long white gloves completed her toilet. Round her neck she wore a single strand of pearls, but no other jewelry. Her hair was caught up with a white ribbon, and more forget-me-nots, the real flowers this time, decorated it. The blue of the flowers exactly matched the startling blue of her eyes. Like some princess out of a fairy tale, she looked white as snow, with hair black as jet, and a delicate coloring with pouting red lips. In the elaborate magnificence of rich materials, smothered with embroidery and jewels, Miranda stood out in simple beauty, just as Lady Eversley had intended she should.

It was clear that she was going to be a social success as soon as she arrived. A mob of young men had crowded round her immediately. Even now, as she rested after a particularly energetic dance, a major in the Lancers was fetching her lemonade, while a young baronet was making earnest conversation about horses in an attempt to win her favor.

"I have just purchased a high flyer, Miss Melbury," he said earnestly, "and a prime pair of chestnuts to draw it. Do you drive a phaeton?"

"I have not yet had the opportunity," said Miranda somewhat wistfully. "My father taught me to ride, of course, but he drew the line at me setting up in my own carriage. Do you think that he was old-fashioned?

There is nothing I should like better than to have my own phaeton."

"Well," said the baronet apologetically, "there's no denying that some of the ladies who drive can be a little vulgar. Take Lady Lade, for instance. She handles the ribbons as well as any man but she don't do much in society. 'Tis said she was friendly with a highwayman before she married Sir John. But you may see *him* everywhere."

"Is he here today," said Miranda with only half an ear to what he was saying. She had just caught sight of a stout elderly-looking man proceeding at a stately pace through the ballroom. At his approach the ladies were curtseying, the men bowing, so that his progress looked like that of a wind, which blew down the grass in front of it. Except that he was so very fat, thought Miranda.

"Who is that fat man over there?" asked Miranda, breaking into her companion's efforts to point out Sir John Lade.

The young baronet looked shocked. "Hush, Miss Melbury," he said. "You must not tease. That is the prince regent. Don't tell me you did not recognize him?"

"I had no idea he looked like that," said Miranda naively. "At Melbury place we always thought of him as a fairytale prince. I did not realize that he was so . . ." she paused, trying not to be offensive, and managed, ". . . so grown in years."

Truly the prince regent was not the dashing royal personage she had been led to expect. Gone was the tall youth who had once signed his letters "Florizel," when wooing a young actress. Once he had played cricket regularly dressed in a white beaver hat, a short flannel jacket with blue ribbon, and close-fitting white trousers.

He had had a string of race horses, and a stud of hunters, and had ridden to hounds with the best of them.

But the man in front of her now was immensely fat. He rarely rode, being too weighty to enjoy that exercise. On his rare ventures on horseback he had to be winched onto the saddle by means of a chair on rollers, pushed up a plank onto a platform, and then let go while the royal prince was deposited onto its saddle. It was very sad, thought Miranda, as she watched him come in her direction.

"There's Sir John, four or five people behind him," said her companion helpfully. "And there's the Earl of Templecombe. Templecombe drives well or better than Sir John. I knew he wouldn't be far away. Prinny won't go to balls unless he knows Templecombe is honoring them with his company."

"Why is it that everybody talks endlessly about the Earl of Templecombe?" said Miranda crossly.

"You obviously do not approve of such a tedious topic. You had best talk to me. I shall not bore you with the subject." The voice was as masterful and confident as ever. It was the Earl of Templecombe who had somehow made his way toward her. "In the meantime let me present you to the prince regent. Michael, may I have this lady's attention for a while?"

"I can't stop you, Templecombe," said the baronet with a grin. "I'm not a good enough swordsman to call you out, otherwise you should answer for such behavior."

Miranda fumed inwardly at this joking exchange. They were treating her as if she was a mere nothing, something to be passed from one man to another. On the other hand she did want to be presented to the prince, and obviously the Earl of Templecombe was just the man to do it.

As she curtseyed low in front of the heir to the throne, she could not help being amazed at the sight of the man who had caused so much public annoyance and disapproval. The Prince of Wales had been a disgraceful spendthrift, pouring hundreds of thousands of pounds into building houses for himself in Carlton Terrace and down at the little village which had once been called Brighthelmstone. He had been hopelessly disliked for his love affairs, too. First he had married poor Mrs. Fitzherbert, a Catholic, in a ceremony that was not binding. Then he had cast her aside in favor of a match arranged by his father. But the Princess of Wales and he had never got on together, and had separated almost immediately. There had been riots in the street in favor of the princess, yet on the other hand Miranda could not help feeling sympathetic toward the prince. It cannot have been very nice being married to a woman who was so severely eccentric.

The prince regent smiled, and took her hand, lifting her up from her low curtsey with a slight cracking noise, which betrayed that corsets were holding in his bulk. "I see you have again picked out a beauty, Templecombe," he said jovially. Miranda did not appreciate the remark. She thought it was in bad taste, but one could hardly show one's disapproval to a royal prince. To her relief, he turned away from her to be presented to another aspirant to the royal favor.

The Earl of Templecombe did not go with him. Instead, he took Miranda's hand and led her formally away to a portion of the ballroom where a lively cotillion was being danced. "I suggest," he said "that we wait until the next dance, which I am reliably informed will be a waltz."

"I should like to dance the cotillion," said Miranda perversely. But at that moment the dance came to an end, and the couples bowed and curtseyed to each other for the final time. "Anyway," she went on, annoyed at being thwarted, "I am surprised that you will dance with me. You were not very polite to me last time we met."

"Does that surprise you, Miss Melbury?" said the earl disagreeably. "Is it not enough that you must have vulgar wagers with your friends, but that you must also dress yourself up as a guttersnipe? Such pranks are not worthy of you. Save them for the rustics. There, perhaps country folk may find them amusing. I do not."

Miranda stood still. She was going to draw her hand from his arm, but to her surprise he took her firmly and led her out onto the dance floor where couples were forming for the waltz.

She knew that, to be consistent, she ought to refuse to dance with him, and yet her whole being longed to. She simply could not bear to give up her chance of dancing with such a splendid partner, and besides, she could see a rustle of interest go round the ballroom as people noticed her partner.

The music struck up. In between vigorous twirls round the room she said, gasping a little, "If you so strongly disapprove of me, Lord Templecombe, why do you want to dance with me?"

"I am anxious that you should not destroy your reputation altogether, Miss Melbury," was the grim response. "I cannot prevent your outrageous pranks, nor. I suspect, can Lady Eversley. But if I continue my interest in you, then perhaps your pranks will be put down as agreeable eccentricities. I can give you countenance. If people think that I am captivated by your charms, then they will think twice before condemning you."

"But why do you want to help me in this way?" persisted Miranda. Naughtily she wanted to hear more. Perhaps the earl really was captivated despite his disapproval. The idea excited her.

"I am not doing it for the sake of your fine eyes, Miss Melbury," he said flatly. "You rate your charms too highly. It is Lady Eversley that I care about. If you shock the polite world with your hoydenish behavior, she will suffer too."

Miranda could not think of anything to say in the face of so comprehensive a snub. She stopped trying to make conversation. It seemed that the earl was disagreeable, whatever she said. Well then, she would remain silent if that was what he wanted. Yet she kept a fixed smile on her face, determined that the world, at least, should not know that they were quarrelling.

Silently they whirled rapidly round the room. Miranda was very conscious of the earl's strong arm round her waist, piloting her through the intricacies of the dance. The waltz brought them very close together, and for the first time Miranda realized why some prudes objected to that closeness. She could feel the earl's strong muscular body, and could smell the slight scent of his snuff.

Without realizing it, she began to melt into the rhythm of the music, giving herself absolutely up to the magic of the evening. It was as if a miraculous power invested her feet with effortless movement. She could feel the strains of the music throbbing through her whole being, as if she was dancing not just with her feet but with her whole body.

Without thinking, she looked up and smiled at her partner, and surprised on his face a look of such unguarded tenderness that it reassured her. He might disapprove of her behavior, but now the waltz had charmed him with its magic, too. He, too, was not thinking of anything other than the beauty of the dance.

As she moved with him round the room, her whole soul was enraptured by a strong emotion—she did not know exactly what. Her heart seemed to be singing within her, and her whole body was light with happiness. The earl and she moved as one being, fused together by the power of music, and made glorious by an unconscious sharing of emotion.

It was with a jolt that she realized that the music had stopped, and that the other couples were bowing and curtseying to each other. She looked up, wanting to say something to the earl, to put into words the magic pleasure she had experienced in his arms. But just at that moment the major in the Lancers came walking up with the lemonade she had so carelessly asked him to procure for her. "My lord," was all she managed to say, in imploring tones.

"I know," he said curtly. "Not now. We will talk later. I hope I shall have the pleasure of another waltz with you, Miss Melbury," he said in a formal tone for the benefit of the young men who were beginning to crowd round her again.

"I should be delighted, Lord Templecombe. We seem well matched on the floor," said Miranda quietly, giving him her best formal curtsey. Then turning to the neglected major, she said: "It is most kind of you to remember my lemonade. I fear I have shockingly forgotten all about it. But I was whisked away by Lord Templecombe to be presented to the prince regent, and we could not resist a waltz. I am sorry if you have had to wait around with that glass very long."

"No sacrifice is too great to win your favor, Miss Melbury," said the major gallantly. "Perhaps my reward can be one of the country dances, which I see are forming."

Miranda smiled at him, and was amused to see that he began to blush. "Of course," she said, and they went to take their places in the dance. But as she moved away, she could not help peeping back to see if the Earl of Templecombe was following her with his eyes. To her annoyance he was not, and yet she felt that somehow even his tall back turned to her expressed a consciousness that she was in the same room. But perhaps it was just her imagination. She tried to give her attention to the gallant major, but failed.

For several dances she passed from one young admirer to another. All of the young men were extremely gallant, and Miranda thought she had never before heard so many compliments. But she found it very difficult to take them all seriously. In her eyes, the young men seemed all so alike, modeling themselves upon the same leader of fashion. So she was not surprised when one of them confided to her: "You know, Miss Melbury, I fancy my neckcloth has the look of one worn by the earl. You've no idea how many hours I have tried to tie one like his, but it never seems to work. But this evening I thought I did pretty well."

"I think so too," said Miranda. Privately, she found it difficult not to laugh. They were all pale shadows of the earl, it seemed. No wonder they struck her as being very similar.

Lady Eversley found time from her *tête à tête* with Mr. Martock to have a few words with her niece. "Wasn't it wonderful the way the earl singled you out again?" she said. "It is much more than I expected." Miranda merely smiled back rather wanly. She decided that she could not tell her aunt now how her feelings had almost overwhelmed her during the waltz. She was chatting to a viscount who was telling her of a new hunter he had purchase, "a bang-up bit of blood," he called it, when a servant came up to her with a note on a silver salver. Miranda begged her chatty companion, "Would you be so kind as to procure me another glass of lemonade while I read this?"

Hurriedly she tore open the mysterious missive, as the viscount lounged off in search of lemonade. To her surprise, it was addressed in an ill-educated hand. *You obedient servant, Mam. I must see you as soon as possibul. I will be hiding in the conservatoy. This is ergent, and a matter of life and deth.*" It was signed *"Betty."*

Miranda did not stop to think of the viscount in search of her lemonade. She realized she must act fast. What on earth was the matter? And how had Betty found her way into the conservatory? She must be desperate, and in terrible trouble . . .

Looking round briefly, Miranda was glad to see that no attention was fixed on her. The guests had crowded round the Duke of Wellington, who had arrived even later than she had. She could slip away now, without anybody noticing. She decided to pretend that her dress was torn, and with an expression of dismay examined the hem. Then quickly, hoping that nobody would detect her, she moved toward the door which led to the conservatory and the back of the house.

The conservatory was lit with candles inside colored lamps, and in their flickering light Miranda could see one or two couples, their faces discreetly turned away from her. She looked round nervously but she could not see Betty anywhere. Then the servant who had brought her the note made his way into the conservatory. "The young person you are waiting for could not gain admittance," he whispered. "You will find her by the gate at the bottom of the garden." With that he turned away rapidly, as if anxious not to be seen communicating with her.

For a moment Miranda stood irresolute. Then she pulled herself together, and opened the door which led out into the moonlit garden. She *must* help Betty. She shivered in the cold night air as she walked through shrubbery. At the bottom of the garden, as the servant had said, there was a small gate which led, no doubt, into the mews. It was shut. Miranda pushed it open cautiously and stepped outside.

As soon as she did so, a large hand came across her mouth, gagging the cry that came to her lips. Huge arms encircled her, and she was lifted off her feet in one move. Desperately she fought against the giant who held her, kicking at his body. But the blows which came from her satin slippers were to no avail. In a kicking bundle, she was carried bodily to a vehicle which was waiting only a few yards away from the gate, and thrust into it.

It was pitch black inside. Her first reaction was to rush to the window and shout for help. But even as she did so, the horses jerked into action, and the vehicle set off at a breakneck speed. A quiet voice from the body of the carriage slid out of the darkness, "Good evening, Miss Melbury."

The cry died on her lips. She turned back to face this new danger. "That's better," said the voice silkily. "You will do well to cease trying to escape. It is impossible my dear, so save your energy for better things."

All at once Miranda realized it was the Beau himself.

He was right. She could not escape. As she hung from the window of the coach, she was nearly sickened by the speed of its journey. To try to jump from it would be certain death on the cobblestones. She sank back into the seat of the coach, as far away as possible from the dark corner. As her eyes became used to the lack of light, she could make out Sir Samuel Brassey's features, from the occasional light cast when the coach rattled by a house whose occupants were still awake.

The coach was driving through the deserted streets at a fearful pace, swinging round the corners as if it was driven by a madman. Miranda found she had to cling to the leather cushions inside the carriage to prevent herself from being toppled into the Beau's arms.

She fought for self-control, and managed to say in a light tone which concealed her fear: "Good evening, Sir Samuel. I hope you will give your coachman orders to stop soon. This joke has gone far enough. If you halt it now, I shall endeavor to forget that it ever happened. I must get back to the ball before my aunt discovers I am missing."

"I could not allow that, Miss Melbury," said Sir Samuel. His voice was agreeable, and he sounded so amiable that he might have been discussing the decoration of a room, or some other pleasant topic, with a hostess at an evening reception. To Miranda's horror he sat forward in his seat and took a pinch of snuff in as collected a way as if he was fulfilling some perfectly normal social engagement.

"Please, Sir Samuel. The scandal will be terrible. I do not wish to elope with you. What can you hope to gain by forcing me in this way?" she said. It was an effort to be conciliating, to stoop to plead with this monster of a man. She made her voice sound pathetic, which was frighteningly easy. "Sir Samuel, I beg of you, if you have the feelings of a gentleman, do let me go."

"My dear," said Sir Samuel, "set your mind at rest.

You are not eloping with me. As you pointed out earlier today, you do not wish to marry me. I shall not force you. I have decided to accept your decision. There is no question of us marrying."

"Where are you taking me, if not Gretna Green?" asked Miranda, trying to keep her voice from trembling. She was bewildered now. She had assumed that the Beau planned a runaway match between them. But if it was not Gretna Green, what could it be? "I am under age, you know," she reminded him. "We cannot be married elsewhere."

"As I said," purred the Beau, "there is no question of marriage between us. I am taking you, my dear Miranda, to the house of a friend of mine at Dover. From there, you and I shall travel in my yacht to the Continent. Once in France, we can become better acquainted. I look forward to that. You and I are going to be the closest of friends, Miranda."

"I do not think so," said Miranda with spirit. She sat bolt upright and looked straight at the man who was so vilely abducting her. "You cannot force me to come with you, nor can you force me to become your mistress. I had rather kill myself than that, do you hear? To be loved by you is to be defiled."

"Dearest girl," said Beau Brassey coolly, taking a pinch of snuff, "you are entirely mistaken. I can and I shall force you. It is only in romances that the heroine chooses death rather than dishonor. You will not have that choice, my beauty. Death is not being offered you. There are many means to force women to obey us men, and I shall not hesitate to use the rougher ones if necessary. But I do not think you will refuse, when you know what will be your fate otherwise."

In the dark Miranda fancied she could almost hear

him smiling. She kept silent, not wishing to give him the satisfaction of knowing how frightened she was. But much of her hope, that he might be somehow persuaded to let her go, died within her. Sir Samuel, it was clear, was *enjoying* her terror. She made one last effort.

"When my aunt misses me, she will send after you," she declared with a conviction she was far from feeling. "And when I denounce you, as I shall unless you set me down immediately, you will be thrown into prison, I've no doubt. There are penalties for abducting minors, as no doubt you know. And my aunt has influence in the highest circles."

"Bravo, Miss Melbury. What spirit you show!" In mockery, the Beau clapped his hands as if applauding her. Miranda could see his face glimmering in the passing lights. It looked elated and full of pleasure at her fear. "Nobody will be pursuing you," he went on. "I have reckoned with that problem and laid plans to stop them. I have left a note, written as if by your own hand, saying that you are flying with me to Gretna Green. The servant whom I bribed to give you that message, will recall how you went willingly to the conservatory. Oh no, I do not think there will be pursuers. But even if there are, they will be following us in the wrong direction. Even so, I do not think your aunt will set out. She will be anxious to leave well enough alone, to damp down the scandal and, if necessary, to accept what she thinks is a romantic marriage."

"How much of this does your cousin, Miss Brassey, know?" asked Miranda desperately.

"Jennifer Brassey? That old spinster? My dear, she is not in my confidence about this . . . er . . . elopement. Why, I have little to do with her. She is scarcely a cousin. I took her from poverty to live with me, and in return she obeys me utterly. Did you think that she knew all my affairs? I assure you she is nothing more than one of the servants . . . less, indeed. For she is worth a great deal less, certainly."

"Did she know of . . . of Floral Street?"

"Jennifer Brassey is a foolish old maid, and I fear she may have poked her nose into my affairs. She had discovered something . . . that is why she took up the Society for the Suppression of Vice. You will understand how much that amused me. I think she thought that in that way she might right any wrongs that I was committing. But she dared do no more. Her livelihood depended upon me."

"What of the blackmailing letter, though?" Miranda was determined, while she could, to discover everything. "Why did she write it?"

Sir Samuel laughed again. "I let you think that we were partners in blackmail," he said. "I had no interest in telling the truth. Jennifer Brassey wrote the letter, 'tis true. She wrote it on my instructions. She dared not do otherwise. It was a way of making sure that I had a hold on her. She and her good works were getting a little . . . shall I say, intrusive. But did you think she had anything to do with the *idea*? She is not capable of that, my dear. No, blackmail was my idea . . . is my idea. You have no idea, my sweetest, what a profitable sideline it is. And the one side of the business . . . the Floral Street business . . . leads so naturally to the other.

"It was excessively amusing to blackmail the aunt while wooing the niece. I assure you that it added spice to the proceedings. I had a strong suspicion that your aunt's lack of ready money would lead her to look favorably upon me as your suitor." He laughed again.

"You will not get away with this abduction, though,"

said Miranda. "Your evil deeds will catch up with you. Unless you release me, there will be a fearful scandal. Surely you do not wish that?"

"I do not care for it. I shall be leaving England for-ever now. I could not stay anyway, for I could not rely on you or your aunt holding your tongues about my . . . er . . . trading interests. So it really has all turned out for the best. I shall take you with me, now that my future lies on the other side of the Channel. I have been trading with France for a long time."

He paused, but Miranda ventured no word. "But I have not told you, my dear, of the alternative which awaits you, should you refuse to be my mistress," he said pleasantly. "Do you wish to know what it is?"

"I have no interest in discussing hypothetical questions," said Miranda stiffly.

"I shall tell you nonetheless," he nevertheless replied. "In France, as you may discover, they are more expert at the business of, what shall I call it? Well, let us say, love. In England we are mainly served in these matters by willing women. True, some of the new entries in our brothels object, but they soon settle down.

"In France, there are great opportunities for enforcement. There are establishments known as closed houses, in which the girls cannot leave. If they run away, the authorities return them, for bribery can accomplish anything. That is your future, Miranda, if you do not submit to me, and if you do not make every effort to please me. I shall not hesitate to put you into one of those establishments, if you fail to give me the fullest satisfaction. I want you to think about this."

His words struck a current of cold fear into Miranda's heart. It seemed like a nightmare, and yet it all fitted in with what she already knew about Beau Brassey. He was not a man who would care anything for morals or decency. Already Miranda knew that he had made money from the ruin and degradation of young girls. Betty Miller's story made that clear. Would he stop short at ruining her? She thought not. She thought he might even enjoy it.

She decided she must fight him with his own weapons of coolness and sarcasm. "It is not an alluring picture that you paint, Sir Samuel," she said in imitation of his own smooth tone. "I wonder that your pride will let you threaten me so. I had thought better of you. The caresses of a slave, and that is what I shall be if your threats are even partly true, surely cannot give you the same satisfaction as those of a woman who has fallen in love with you."

He looked admiringly at her. "You are so intelligent, my dear. I never cease to marvel at your courage and your charms. I assure you that I would prefer to win your love. But equally if I cannot win your love by fair means, I am willing to try foul. I am not a romantic. Besides, I should find, perhaps, a curious pleasure in seeing you confronted with the life of a brothel. It would be interesting to see whether you could retain your innocence of mind in such a situation.

"In fact, it could be a little experiment, to see how far your intelligence and your wit, and your undoubted beauty, could withstand such a life. Usually the girls do not last long. Their careers lead downward, not upward, and the last part of their working life is usually spent in the docks area of Paris or in Marseilles.

"It is not an easy life. Some even die. I wonder what your fate would be. Perhaps your intelligence would enable you to withstand the depressing aspects of such an exhausting life. On the other hand, it might make the life harder to endure. I shall not shock you by telling you how many customers the girls in the ports are expected to entertain during an evening."

Miranda put her hands to her ears to cut out that insidious voice. His words, she knew, were calculated to terrify her, and yet she did not think that Sir Samuel was bluffing. He was much, much more of a villain than either she or her aunt had realized. She shuddered.

The Beau must have seen that movement. He moved from his seat toward her, until she could feel his thigh pressing against hers. Unconsciously, she shrank back into the leather seat in the corner of the coach, although she could not escape him that way.

Desperately, as he moved nearer again, she glanced out of the window in order to calculate whether she might throw herself upon the paving stones. But the vehicle was going at such a frightful pace, that it would probably be fatal. Death rather than dishonor, thought Miranda wildly.

Then she pulled herself together. She must not panic yet. There was still a chance, if not a big one, that her aunt or somebody might be in pursuit. She must not give way to utter despair yet. But even as this passed through her mind, she made a vow to kill herself rather than face the horrors of which the Beau spoke. Death would be infinitely preferable and there were many ways to die. . . .

As if he had read her mind, the man beside her gave a low laugh. "You cannot throw yourself out of the coach yet, Miranda. You must wait. Perhaps your friends are on their way to rescue you. You must wait, my pretty, while I amuse myself." As he spoke the jeering words, he put his arm round her.

Instinctively, she pulled herself free from his embrace, and without thinking twice rounded upon him and slapped his face. The blow resounded above the rattle of the carriage. Her hand tingled from the strength of it, for she had put her whole force behind it. In the dim light, she could see an angry weal on his face, left by her stinging fingers. The Beau had gone pale with fury and had jerked away from her. He said nothing, but as Miranda watched the mark of her hand glowing red on his pallid cheeks, she was suddenly absolutely terrified.

He moved toward her again. This time, instead of putting his arm around her, he seized her hands in his, and forced them behind her back. She was thus pinioned by him, and he gloated at her dismay. "You will apologize on your knees one day for that blow, Miss Melbury," he said quietly, still with the silky smile on his lips. "And now I shall have that kiss I promised myself. I shall have more. I can see that the sooner you admit I am master, the better."

His lips came down on hers when he finished speaking, and he clamped his hot, wet mouth onto hers. It was like the embrace of a poisonous snake, thought Miranda, as she twisted and turned, unable to evade his loathesome caress. No matter how much she pulled, she could not release her wrists from his grasp.

It seemed an endless torment. Then he took his mouth away. "I am going to be sick," cried Miranda, and involuntarily her body began to heave. This weakened his grasp, and she was able to tear her wrists away from his hands. As she bent sickly over the seat, her body heaving, gasping for breath, she was trying to think calmly. "I promise you if you will not . . . make love to me . . . I shall not try to escape," she managed to say.

A chuckle was the only reply he vouchsafed. "That was but a beginning, sweetheart," he taunted. "You must find a better promise than that. I shall give you lessons in loving, do not fear. Such innocence will be a pleasure to teach."

He lunged toward her again with his whole body, with such a force that she collapsed back against the seat. Hot wet kisses rained down on her mouth and her eyes, and his hands seemed to be everywhere. Miranda heard the soft muslin of her dress tear in his beastly grasp.

With a desparing cry, she tried to clasp the remnants of the thin material in front of her to hide her nakedness. The Beau roughly pulled away her covering arms.

She felt so much loathing and so much fear that the intensity of her emotions blotted out everything else. The rattling carriage, and the man struggling to close in on her . . . it all began to waver in front of her eyes, till a merciful unconsciousness blotted it all out.

9

A squeal of wheels and a horrifying crashing noise brought her to her senses. The whole side of the coach seemed to come toward her. She was flung to the ground, and the heavy body of the Beau cannoned on top of her, pushing the breath quite out of her body with the shock.

Darkness and confusion reigned. Miranda could not think what on earth could have happened. The coach had obviously been flung on its side. Now she could see the dark sky and stars glimmering from the top of the door on its uppermost side.

The Beau had moved off her, and she could hear him cursing, using words that even Sir Peter, a hard-riding gentleman, would never have soiled his lips with. Paying no attention to her, he had struggled to his feet, and was climbing over her body in an attempt to open the door above their heads.

Miranda lay there, silently. She had not screamed as the coach crashed, and though she was bruised, she remained still. She hoped Sir Samuel would assume that she had not regained consciousness. It seemed safer than letting him know she had regained her senses.

With relief she heard him mutter: "The girl is still

out cold. Oh well, she must stay while I right things."
Then her heart gave a leap of gratitude and relief as he
painfully pushed open the door, and in an ungainly fashion hauled himself out of it. She could hear his body
slither down the side of the coach to the ground.

For a second she lay recruiting her strength. Now or
never was her chance to escape. Painfully she tried to
stand upright, and succeeded. But she winced as she
placed her weight on her right ankle. It hurt like a hot
brand, and fiery shoots of pain darted through it. She
must have fallen upon it in the crash and sprained or
wrenched it. It was the worst time to have a sprain,
thought Miranda. Now her chances of escape were much
less. She might well haul herself out of the coach, but
with the pain crippling her she could never hope to out-
distance pursuers.

In the darkness of the coach, she could not tell what
ravages Beau Brassey had wrought upon her ballroom
finery. She could only tell that he must have torn the
bodice. Womanlike, she tried to rearrange its tattered
remnants into a decent covering before she attempted
escape. Then, standing tiptoe despite the pain in her
ankle, she peered out the open door.

She was completely astounded at what she saw. She
hauled herself up, supporting herself with her hands, so as
to get a better view. The moonlight was strong, and cast
everything into a silvery light. The coach had succeeded
in reaching one of the main roads out of London toward
the coast, and it had come to grief on a deserted piece of
commonland somewhere on the outskirts of the capi-
tal city. Miranda could see houses in the distance, but
none were near enough for her to count on the inhabi-
tants' aid.

But what puzzled her most was the sight of the Beau.

Sir Samuel was standing, with his back to her, his whole attention centered on somebody or something else. Miranda could not see properly who or what.

She decided she must make some effort to at least get out of the coach while his attention was thus engaged. At the very worst her situation could hardly be made more dangerous. If only she could slip out while the Beau was not looking in her direction, then perhaps a miracle would occur and she might get a chance to flee.

Painfully she clambered out of the coach, and slithered down its side to the ground. She made quite a noise doing it, or so it seemed to her, but the Beau did not even turn in her direction. Limping, she tried to run across the road, with the idea that she might at least throw herself behind some of the little thorn bushes dotted over the rough grazing of the common.

"Ah, Miss Melbury. Where are you going?" came a familiar voice. It was icily polite as usual. Miranda jerked round, and saw the tall figure of a man holding a pistol trained on Sir Samuel Brassey's heart.

It was the Earl of Templecombe.

Astounded, she did not answer, but just gaped at him, utterly confused by the turn events were taking. Here was the true reason for Sir Samuel's fixed attention —a dueling pistol pointing straight at him.

"You do not seem very pleased to see me, Miss Melbury," said the earl. "Could it be because I have put an end to your elopement? I suspect that you thought this was a romantic notion. Let me tell you, Miss Melbury, that a clandestine flight like this can only ruin your reputation forever."

Miranda still said nothing. She could not believe her ears.

The earl went on. "You are more fortunate than you

think, Miss Melbury. I was astonished to see that your carriage was not taking the Great North Road toward Scotland. You are no doubt ignorant of Sir Samuel's plans, but he appears to be making for the coast. Perhaps you are too much of a country miss to know that. Or was your intention to fling everything to the winds, and gallivant off to France with him?"

Miranda looked at Sir Samuel. A slight smile played round his thin lips. Before she could say anything, he broke into the conversation. "You are no doubt hurt, Templecombe, that the lady preferred my addresses to yours. But you may not know that we were formally engaged. Only twenty-four hours ago Miss Melbury and I plighted our troth. We were on our way to Paris and a Continental honeymoon. So romantic, don't you think?"

The earl ground his teeth with rage. "Is it true?" he asked Miranda grimly.

"It's *not* true," said Miranda in a voice of utter panic. "Please believe me, Lord Templecombe. I am being abducted. I am desperately thankful you have rescued me. I never meant to get engaged to Sir Samuel. It was all a terrible mistake."

The earl glanced at her. "So you admit you were engaged," he said. As he looked, his guard wavered, and his attention was on her.

"Be careful," cried Miranda. She saw Beau Brassey move with the lightning swiftness of a snake. That second's grace given to him by the wavering of the earl's attention was enough. From his coat he pulled out a pearl-handled pistol, and the sound of a shot rang out.

Simultaneously a burst of flame came from the gun's barrel, and the earl sprang back. But he did not return the fire. "I warn you, Sir Samuel, my bullet will be in your heart. Throw down your pistol."

With a curse, the Beau flung down the smoking pistol into the dust at his feet. "Come, Templecombe," is all he said. "I will challenge you. I demand satisfaction."

"It is my right to demand satisfaction," said the earl through grim lips. "But 'tis enough. We will fight." Even as he spoke, Miranda for the first time noticed a dark stain spreading from his left shoulder. It was blood. Sir Samuel's bullet had not gone wide.

"You cannot fight, Lord Templecombe," she cried. "You are wounded, man! Cannot you see that Sir Samuel will play foul? He has nothing to lose."

The earl laughed. "A mere flesh wound, my dear. I should have thought it would add to the interest of the duel for you. What, faint-hearted? This is not the fearless Miss Melbury I have met before."

Miranda sank to her knees in the dust. From out of the corner of her eye she could see the coachman and a groom looking with wondering faces on the scene that was being enacted before them. She wondered why they had not come to their master's rescue, and then concluded that they dared make no move while a pistol was pointing at his heart.

. "Please, Lord Templecombe," she beseeched him. "I beg you. Do not trust Sir Samuel with a duel. He is no gentleman. He is a desperate man and will surely kill you by fair means or foul. At least make sure that he has no servants to aid him. Send these away." She gestured at the two men.

"I will obey your last command," said the earl mockingly. "Off you go, my fellows," he ordered the servants. "Else I will put a bullet through the heart of your master in front of your very eyes." As he hesitated, the earl took careful aim, and Miranda could not help gasping as she saw him tightening his finger on the trigger.

Obviously the two servants shared her apprehension, for after a muttered consultation, they set off down the road in the direction of London. Miranda saw Sir Samuel's eyes narrow, and his brow furrow, as he saw them go. From the look on his face, he would have given a large slice of his fortune to call them back, but he dared not do so while the deadly weapon was pointing at his heart.

"Now, Sir Samuel," said the earl, as they had gone several hundred yards. "Do you have a sword in the coach?"

"There is one there," said the Beau eagerly. "Shall I get it?"

"Don't move," warned the earl. "I am not minded to suffer a second bullet or some other treachery from you. Miss Melbury will fetch your weapon. But first, my dear" —the endearment was sneeringly offered—"perhaps you would make yourself useful by relieving your betrothed of that pistol on the ground."

Without replying to the sneer, Miranda obeyed him. She gingerly picked up the weapon.

"Bring it over here," ordered the earl. "No, girl, don't point it at me, or at yourself. Point it at the ground. Now take the pistol that I am holding and keep it steady in this direction." He moved aside, so that she stood in his place, holding the pistol aimed at Sir Samuel's heart.

As she stood there, she thought she saw a change in Sir Samuel's expression. "I should certainly squeeze the trigger," she said to him coolly. "It would give me considerable pleasure to kill you, Sir Samuel. I should not risk it, if I was you. I am not a bread-and-butter miss who will faint at any loud noise."

As she spoke, the earl was examining the Beau's pistol. Satisfied that there was no possibility of its being fired again, he tossed it high into the air toward the common. While Miranda still held the pistol, he walked casually over to the Beau, being careful not to put himself in the way of her aim. "I will make sure that you do not have the twin of that pistol still on you," he said, as he went through the pockets of the Beau's coat.

"Templecombe, I believe you are in as much danger as I am from Miss Melbury at the moment," said the Beau. "I marvel at your courage."

"There is something in what you say," replied the earl with a grim smile. "But you would not escape, I assure you. I should break your neck first." With these unlovely words, he strolled back to Miranda, and took the pistol away from her, still keeping Sir Samuel in its aim.

"Now get the sword from the coach," he said.

"May I not bind up your wound first," she asked. The dark stain was spreading farther down his coat, and although he showed no signs of being affected by it, she feared that he could not win a duel in his condition. It was only his left shoulder, but the loss of blood must eventually tell on even his superhuman strength.

"Do as I bid you," was all that the earl said. Fearing to annoy him, or divert his full attention from Sir Samuel by arguing, she made her way back to the coach to search for the sword. She had to scramble back in, but she found it, with difficulty, at the bottom of the coach among the jumbled leather cushions.

"Here it is," she said, flashing the metal in the air, as she made her way back to the two men. "Shall I give it to Sir Samuel?"

"Not yet," ordered the earl. "First you can help me with my wound. Do you have anything with which I can make a pad?"

Miranda thought for a moment. "There is my petticoat," she said rather doubtfully. "My dress is ruined, so it can hardly matter if I tear a strip off the petticoat, too."

The earl gave her a quick appraising glance, as if noticing her torn frock for the first time. "The petticoat will do nicely," he said.

Without hesitation, Miranda sat down at the side of the road. It was no time for ladylike shrinking, but she could not help blushing slightly as she cautiously lifted her skirt a little way. Using both hands, she managed to tear a large strip off her petticoat.

The Beau was watching her. "What an enticing sight, Miss Melbury," he sneered. "It would no doubt inflame my senses, were not that pistol aimed at me. What a fascinating tale I shall have to tell my friends. But then perhaps I will win the duel, and we shall enjoy our Continental honeymoon together, my charmer."

His words made Miranda's blood curdle with horror. Worse still, she realized that Lord Templecombe may have thought that the Beau's familiar words sprang from some kind of shared intimacy in the coach. She could not help a deeper blush, but she said nothing. It was no time for explanations. She folded the torn strip of material into a pad and offered it to the earl.

For the second time he passed the pistol to her and helped her aim it accurately at the Beau. She thought, with fear, that the earl was a little paler than before. Perhaps the wound was tiring him. While she stood there, the pistol aimed at her abductor's heart, she could not help wondering whether perhaps the easiest thing to do would be simply to squeeze the trigger, and save the earl from the duel.

Sir Samuel must have seen the thought flicker across her face, for he said: "You know, my charmer, that you would have the devil of a lot of explaining to do if you shot me down like a dog. You would be acquitted, no doubt, but I wonder if your aunt would ever recover from seeing her niece in the dock of the Old Bailey on trial for murder."

The earl, at Miranda's side, gave a snort of laughter. He had succeeded in fixing the pad underneath his coat, and for a moment the dark stain was halted. "Come now, Sir Samuel, there is no need to fear Miss Melbury. She is not going to kill you. I am." He picked up the sword that Miranda had left on the ground, and flung it over to land at the Beau's feet. At the same time, he withdrew his own weapon from its sheath.

"I will leave the pistol with you, Miss Melbury," he said. "Should anything happen to me, you may need it. You will find my horse tethered over there. Use it to escape. But I beg of you to be careful. Do not point that pistol at either of us while we are fighting, no matter what seems to be happening. Otherwise you may well end up injuring me, rather than Sir Samuel."

"As well leave a lighted tinder near a barrel of gunpowder," jeered Sir Samuel. As Miranda lowered the pistol so that it no longer pointed at him, he picked up the sword at his feet, twitched back his cuffs in readiness, and took up a fencer's position. "On guard, Templecombe."

The two men gave the briefest of salutes, then their swords clashed in the first exchanges of the fight.

It made an extraordinary scene, two well-dressed figures fighting, out in a moonlit night. The silver beams glinted on the blades of their weapons and cast their dark shadows like giants on the dusty road. Sir Samuel was dressed in elegant breeches and a jacket suitable for traveling. The earl was still in the black formal knee breeches and cutaway coat that he had worn to Lady Jersey's ball.

Miranda stood near the coach, twisting her hands in

an agony of fear, as she watched them. She looked round desperately to see if she might run somewhere for aid, but could see no sign of life, except the far-off retreating figures of the coachman and the groom, who were plodding their way toward London.

The two men fought fiercely. On the point of height and weight the earl had the advantage. He was more powerfully built than the Beau. But, unlike his opponent, he had already been wounded and Miranda thought she noticed just a hint of stiffness in the way that he fought. Thank goodness, she thought, that it had only been his left arm that had been wounded.

Sir Samuel Brassey was no mean opponent. Though less strongly built than the earl, he was light on his feet, and his weapon flickered and flashed in the moonlight like a lizard's tongue. It probed, always searching for a weak spot in the earl's guard, and aiming all his efforts at the already wounded shoulder.

Miranda gasped as he feinted toward the earl, withdrew his blade unexpectedly, then pushed it through the earl's guard in one swift motion toward the earl's heart. The earl checked, and, just in the nick of time, countered with a blow that took the blade off its fatal course.

It was clear that he was beginning to weaken. As far as Miranda could make out in the moonlight, his wound had begun to bleed again, seeping through the pad she had fashioned of her petticoat. There was a strained expression on his face. His guard remained faultless, his blade flashing in such a way as to put a ring of steel round him. Yet it could not go on. . . .

As if sensing this, Sir Samuel began to step up his attacks, fearlessly testing the earl's defenses at every point, and always, Miranda noticed, making swordplay that required the earl to move that wounded shoulder in defense.

The Beau was literally playing with the earl's weakness, his whole attention centered on making the dark blood ooze from the coat. It was terrible to watch his catlike concentration on the wound of his opponent. He might not be able to get through the earl's guard yet, but he could draw off his lifeblood.

Suddenly there was a passage of arms so fast that Miranda could not see which blade was involved. All she knew was that at the end of it, the earl staggered back panting a little, for a moment at a loss.

"Have at you, Templecombe," shouted the Beau with elation. He pressed forward for the kill. "My hit, I think."

Somehow the earl countered him. "You have not won yet," he gasped, as he fought off his opponent.

With a heroic effort, the earl reversed the position. Up till now it was the Beau who had been doing all the attacking. Now Miranda could not help a gasp of admiration. Though the Beau had just slashed the earl on his left arm so that a new trickle of blood joined the larger stain, he was not daunted. The earl had leaped to the attack. He pressed it home to the Beau, with a marvelous display of swordsmanship. Sir Samuel fought back with skill and patience, countering the increasingly savage thrusts with no mean skill. But for the first time Miranda began to see that the earl, despite his wounds, was the better swordsman. He seemed everywhere. At one moment Miranda though the end had come for him. His blade had thrust forward, only to be countered by the Beau in such a way as though it would be wrenched from his hand. But with a curious change of direction, the earl managed to keep control of his weapon. His wound seemed to make no difference to his iron control and tireless muscles. He kept on attacking, so that the Beau found himself stepping back several paces to ward off the fury of the earl's assault.

Then the blade flashed forward, checked to meet Beau Brassey's counterthrust, and continued on its way right into the other man's right side. The Beau fell back into the dust. Blood was pouring from a wound on his left side. He was struggling for breath.

For a moment, the earl paused, leaning heavily on his sword. It was obvious that the last magnificent attack had cost him dear. He was almost spent. "I have not touched the heart," he gasped to Miranda. "I do not think he will die. But it will be some time before he decides on another elopement."

Miranda came forward from the shadows where she had been breathlessly watching the two men. She knelt down by the Beau, and felt his pulse. Sir Samuel Brassey's eyes were closed, and he was lying totally still, but his pulse was quite strong. "He is not dead yet," she said. "Must we find him help, or can we leave him here? I have no wish to see him recover."

The earl gave a grim little laugh. "So bloodthirsty about your former admirer, Miss Melbury? We will leave him here, but we will send back his servants. They can look after him."

As he spoke, he swayed dangerously, as if he was about to faint. Then he pulled himself together, still using his sword for support.

"You are badly hurt yourself," cried Miranda and ran up to him. She was about to look at the wound on his shoulder, when he motioned to her to desist.

"It's a mere scratch, my dear," he said. "The Beau's sword has not hurt me much. But his bullet goes a thought deeper. I daresay I shall recover, but how the devil am I going to get you back to your home tonight?"

Privately, Miranda thought that a question of equal difficulty was how on earth she was going to get *him* back. But she did not say anything aloud, contenting herself with demanding: "Will your horse carry two of us?"

"It must, my dear." He pointed to the scrubby bush to which the steed was tethered, quietly munching the grass, its bit jangling as it ate. Running over to it, Miranda untied the beast and led it toward the earl.

"If I get on first, do you think you could manage to mount behind me? Then I shall ride it back. You must hang onto my waist," she said firmly. Now it was her turn to give the orders.

For a second, it looked as if the earl would object, but in the end he merely laughed. "I had forgot that you are a bruising rider," he muttered mockingly. "Well, then, Miss Melbury, you had best show your skill, for by God's sake, it is I who need *your* help now. I fear neither of us shall get home this night, unless you can take the reins."

With the lightness of years of practice, Miranda mounted the large horse. It was a noble animal, fit for a man to ride, rather than a ladies' mount. It was not easy for her to manage astride with her petticoats, but somehow she managed it. She had to pause to adjust the stirrups so that she could put her feet in them. Then she arranged her skirts so that the leathers should not bruise her too severely.

Getting the earl to mount behind her proved difficult. Despite several efforts, he could not pull himself to the saddle. His wounded shoulder would not allow it. His grimly set mouth showed that it pained him severely. Eventually, at Miranda's suggestion, he managed to climb on behind her by way of mounting from the side of the wrecked coach. Once he was safely up and clasping her waist with both his arms, she gave a last look at the body of Sir Samuel. "He looks like a corpse," she said, not without relish.

"He's no corpse. I should know. I didn't aim to kill, just to disable him," said the earl thickly from behind her. Despite his wound, his arrogance, she noticed, was still in evidence.

Slowly the big horse started forward. From the pressure of his body behind her, Miranda could sense that the earl was hurt by the trotting of the horse. He said nothing but his arms around her waist tightened, as if his body was bracing itself against the shocking pain. Yet it would take too long if they were to walk. There was only one solution, thought Miranda, and that was to canter.

She waited until they had caught up with the coachman and groom, and told them about their wounded master. The two men looked dismayed, as if they would as soon not bother to return, but one look at the fierce face of the man behind Miranda and they reluctantly started back where they had come from.

Miranda urged the horse to a canter. The sound of its hooves echoed in the quiet streets as they made their way back into the huge wen of the metropolis. Most of the houses were shuttered and barred against the night. Occasionally in some humble dwelling a tallow light flickered as a cobbler worked late into the small hours, or some half-starved milliner counted her weary stitches.

Once, a tabby cat streaked across their path, causing the big horse to swerve alarmingly. Miranda kept her seat without difficulty, but she felt the man behind her sway dangerously in the saddle. His arms were still clasped round her waist, but his body fell forward against her back as if he had lost consciousness.

She did not dare look round, instead concentrated on keeping the powerful gray horse up to its pacing. But she could feel a sinister dampness against her right shoulder, where the earl's warm blood was oozing out onto the white muslin of her ballgown.

That mad night's gallop through the deserted streets seemed to go on forever. Always she was conscious that behind her was a severely wounded, perhaps even a dying, man. His lifeblood was slowly draining away as each minute passed.

She was not sure which way to take, but as the houses became more frequent she was relieved to recognize the narrow streetways of the City of London. She could see the dome of St. Paul's in front of her, and then behind her. There were occasional figures of people going about what must be unlawful business, now that they were in the center of the town. She was worried when she thought about footpads, highwaymen, and other denizens of the night who might try to hold her up. Yet she had to stop to ask the way more than once, else risk losing her way. When she stopped, she kept the big gray horse well away from her informant, so that no footpad might drag her or the earl out of the saddle.

It was a frightful journey. At last, shivering with fear and cold, she saw the familiar houses of Eaton Square. As she tumbled out of the saddle at her aunt's house, the man behind her fell forward in a dead faint. She had to leave the big horse standing there, his flanks heaving, his reins trailing in the road, and his master fallen into unconsciousness on his back.

She tore up the steps to ring the bell. "Quick, Stratton," she gasped at the sleepy-eyed butler who came to the door. "Get help to the earl. He is wounded. Be quick man," she cried at him. "There is no time to lose."

Somehow servants materialized from the bowels of the house, she did not know how. She saw Helmslow come from somewhere in the mews where he must have been waiting for her return. He lifted off the limp body of her rescuer, while another groom led away the horse. She glimpsed Lady Eversley at the top of the stairs, and Miss Dunn behind her making a disapproving murmur.

But it was all a muddle of sights and sounds, such was her reaction from the events of the night. Somehow somebody put her to bed, she remembered later. And that night, though she fell asleep, it did not seem like slumber. Instead it was like falling into a pit of a nightmare, in which the sound of horses' hooves through empty streets echoed endlessly, while blades flashed in the moonlight, and through everything blood oozed out in a warm wet stain.

10

The midday sun was casting its strong golden beams through the heavy silk curtains when Miranda woke. It was late morning. For a moment she could not think where she was. Downstairs there was the hum of the household going about its duties. Outside, instead of the familiar bird song of Melbury Place, there was the bustle of traffic and the footsteps of hundreds of people going about their daily business in the streets of London.

Miranda could hear a girl singing. Perhaps it was the Knightsbridge milkmaid plying her wares round the streets, or perhaps a milliner delivering one of her creations to its new owner. The song was a popular one at Vauxhall Gardens, where Mrs. Weichsell, one of the favorite female stars, was every night begged to favor the company with "Know Your Mind."

As Miranda lay there, she could just make out the words . . .

To know your own Mind when you mean to be kind,—
Dear Ladies, a task the most easy to learn.
Then know your own Mind, when a Shepherd you find,
Who your Passion with Honor and Love will return.

She lay in the large bed, thinking, while the words of the song faded slowly out of earshot. The girl was on her way. Miranda sighed. Suddenly, with the clarity of a beam of sunlight, there came a new idea. She had known all along in the back of her mind, but now she knew for certain.

She was in love.

And the object of her love was none other than the man whose limp body she had last seen being hauled off his horse—the Earl of Templecombe.

Lying there, with the sunlight filling up the room and the bustle of daytime outside in the street, Miranda puzzled at how it had happened. It was as if the final piece of a jigsaw had suddenly been slotted into place. Now that the whole picture was clear to her, it was difficult to see how she could have been so slow to realize. She had loved the earl for quite some days.

And yet, when she had first met him, in that horrid encounter in the country lane, she could have sworn she had taken a dislike to the arrogant nobleman who had behaved so badly. The time, too, when he danced with her at her coming-out ball, she had felt uplifted, but she had thought the excitement had come simply from waltzing. She had failed to understand that it was the man in whose arms she had been twirling who had made her heart beat so strongly. If somebody had asked her after that dance whether she liked the Earl of Templecombe she would have hotly denied it. After all, their conversation had been more of a sparring match than the sweet nothings of two people who were attracted. She had, if anything, felt angered by his careless goodwill and the effortless way in which he had made her fashionable.

Then she thought of Sir Samuel Brassey. At that same occasion, Sir Samuel had undoubtedly been more polite than the earl. He had sugared his conversation with elaborate courtesies and compliments. Yet his soft words had concealed a black heart. His appearance might have been amiable, yet it was he, rather than the earl, who had turned out to be such a shocking hand with women. The Earl of Templecombe might be a rake, but he had certainly never degraded or made money out of females in the way that Sir Samuel had done.

When had Miranda's hatred of the earl turned to love? Or had it been love all along, wondered Miranda. With a blush she remembered the rapture she had felt at Lady Jersey's ball. The experience of being in his arms for those few minutes had been amazingly beautiful in a way which seemed to have nothing to do with the kind of pleasure that Sir Samuel's compliments had given her. Miranda sighed with the magic recollection. She had experienced, for those moments at least, some of the joy of being in love. Her heart had known, even then, that this was the man, the only man, whom she could love.

She could not help shuddering when she thought how she had engaged herself to marry Sir Samuel. How could she have been so foolish? Why on earth had she not understood that it was the earl who held the keys to her heart?

Thank God, he had finally rescued her from Sir Samuel. The horror of the abduction was just too terrible for memory to dwell on. She tried to put it out of her mind. Worse still was the recollection of the wounded man who had saved her and whose lifeblood had been seeping away on that midnight gallop back to London. She must not think of it ...

Instead, she tried to remember what the earl had said earlier. If she remembered rightly he must have pursued the coach, when it set out from Lady Jersey's ball. He must have thought that she had consented to elope with Sir Samuel. Seeing it go off in the direction of Dover, he had thought perhaps that the Beau had deceived her about marriage, and had gone to the rescue. He was not to know that the deception had started even earlier, and that only a ruse had made her get into the coach. It had not been possible to explain fully. She had told him that Sir Samuel was abducting her, but did he believe her? Appearances were certainly against it. She had apparently left the ball-room willingly enough. The earl was not to know that the note which had been handed to her was a trick.

It was such a muddle! After he had been wounded and fought the duel, there had been only one thing to do: ride as fast as the wind back for help. Fortunately, thought Miranda, she was a good rider. Sir Peter's up-bringing had ensured that. The thousands of hours she had spent in the saddle had probably saved the earl's life.

For a second, as they had been waltzing together the night before, she had wondered if the earl loved her. She had thought she sensed some emotion in him. But even if he cared *then*, he could surely care no longer. The earl, everybody agreed, had his pride. He would never love a lady who had eloped (as it must seem to him) with a rival.

And yet . . . supposing she was to ask Lady Eversley to explain everything, tell the earl about the blackmailing attempts of Sir Samuel, then surely the earl might under-stand what had really happened. It is my only chance, thought Miranda desperately. Obviously this is what she must do. It was no good just letting love slip by without an attempt to win the heart of the man she loved. Aunt Dorothy would surely understand. She would realize that Miranda's whole happiness was at stake.

Miranda got out of bed and dressed. It was with a cheerful countenance, therefore, that she made her way down the main staircase toward the morning room. The day was a new one, after all. There was still hope—if only Aunt Dorothy would confess to the earl.

As soon as she opened the door, she realized that she had interrupted a private *tête à tête*. Lady Eversley and Mr. James Martock, middle-aged as they both were, sprang apart, both wearing ludicrously guilty expressions

"Good morning, Miss Melbury," said Mr. Martock with a blushing bow, "I trust you are in health this morning. I was just asking your aunt if she would accompany me to the *ridotto* on Saturday. I hoped I might gallant you both there."

Lady Eversley broke in on her lover's well-meaning but unsuccessful effort, to conceal his embarrassment. "Dearest Miranda," she said, "we are both so happy. James and I are going to be married. Isn't it wonderful?"

Mr. James Martock gave a positively boyish smile that lightened up his otherwise serious face. "Your aunt is right to tell you. Why should we hide our happiness? She is going to make me the happiest man in the world and, if I may say so, I shall be delighted to be . . . your uncle, Miranda. Please look on me from now on as a close relative."

Miranda made an exclamation of happiness, and rushed across the room to embrace her aunt. "Dearest Aunt Dorothy, I know you will both be very happy. I am so glad for you. When are you going to announce your engagement?"

"Just as soon as I can pen the advertisement for *The Gazette*," said Mr. Martock, grinning. "I am not a young man and so I am anxious not to waste any more time than

I need in the single state. I only hope I can persuade your aunt that delay is fruitless and that we should complete the ceremony as soon as ever may be."

"Dearest James," sighed Lady Eversley, relaxing gracefully as he strode across the room and took her in his arms. "You know, dear Miranda, you have no idea how blissful it is to be *courted* again. Of course, I am looking forward to being married, but I cannot pretend that I am not enjoying the sensation which precedes the actual ceremony."

"I swear I shall always court you, dearest," said Mr. Martock tenderly.

They made a touching picture of middle-aged happiness, thought Miranda, and her eyes misted over slightly. She could not help sighing as she thought of how she would like to be in their place with the earl.

"You will make your home with us, dearest Miranda," her aunt said firmly.

"I am not sure," said Miranda thoughtfully. "I am not sure what I shall do at the moment." She suddenly realized that she could not ask her aunt to risk her happiness by confessing to the earl. Suppose the earl took it into his head to tell Mr. Martock. It could only lead to trouble.

"Oh," shrieked Lady Eversley suddenly, "I am so scatterbrained that I forgot to ask you about last night, Miranda. Can you forgive me? I must hear at once, child, about your frightful ordeal. Why, I was agog with horror and curiosity until James's proposal drove it from my mind."

Lady Eversley's sudden change from blissful love to horrified concern made her niece want to laugh. There was no doubt that her older female relative was a scatterbrain. "I will tell you," said Miranda, settling herself on the settee, and bracing herself for the narration. "Only I am afraid that you will be very much shocked. And I must beg Mr. Martock not to tell a soul what I am now going to reveal."

The two lovers sat down, one on either side of her, and without mentioning anything about the blackmail, Miranda told the incredible story of the last evening's events. To her own ears, it sounded as if there was rather a gap in the explanation of how she had been lured to the conservatory, but Mr. Martock, if he noticed it, was far too well-bred to inquire further. Besides, his attention seemed mainly engaged in gazing at Lady Eversley in a besotted manner.

She had merely explained about Sir Samuel Brassey's disgraceful behavior in the coach, when Lady Eversley suddenly broke in. "What a terrible scandal this will cause if it gets out, Miranda," she gasped. "It must be hushed up. How can we ensure that Beau Brassy does not breathe a word?"

Although she did not say more, Miranda thought she could read between the lines of her aunt's remarks. Lady Eversley obviously did not want to say anything about Beau Brassey's blackmail attempt lest Mr. Martock know about it.

"Dearest Aunt," said Miranda, choosing her words carefully, "do not be anxious. Nobody shall hear anything about Sir Samuel from me. I will be silent as the grave. I can be trusted." She added, "Nor will the Earl of Templecombe reveal anything." And she told how the earl had so courageously intervened, his fight with Sir Samuel, the wound, and that last terrifying gallop through the deserted streets back to safety.

"He will not die," she said. "I do not think that either the bullet wound or the sword wound was deep enough.

And that really is the end of my history. It has all the trappings of romance, except that I have not fallen into the arms of the hero at the end of it. Indeed, I do not imagine the earl will trouble himself anymore with me, for he seemed disgusted by the whole imbroglio," she could not help adding.

Lady Eversley looked at her niece with a curiously intense gaze for a moment. "The earl said he was disgusted? Could you not have explained the truth to him?"

"I told him that Sir Samuel had abducted me, and that I had not gone willingly, but why should he believe me?" said Miranda bitterly. Unspoken was her own thought that the only thing which made sense of Sir Samuel's extraordinary behavior was his involvement in blackmailing. And that she could not tell the earl, not could she even mention it in front of Mr. Martock, who was sitting on her left.

"I fear that the earl already thinks me a hoyden. He has told me I am lost to all sense of propriety," she said rather forlornly. "I cannot think that this latest adventure will make him change his mind."

"Well, never mind, dear," said her aunt, still in a slightly odd tone of voice. "It is not as if you were fond of him. You had an agreeable flirtation, that was all."

"I suppose so." Even to her own ears Miranda's voice sounded lacking in conviction. I must not show what I really feel, she resolved. She therefore managed to add: "He is an odiously rude man."

"That's odd," put in Mr. Martock. "Templecombe is usually civil enough to me. At least, I have always found him so. He is usually as smooth as butter to the ladies. Too smooth, my sister says. I am surprised that he has been rude to you, Miss Melbury. My sister says he is a great deal too charming usually to young women, though I must confess that is the sort of thing she *would* say."

"So what will you do now?" broke in Lady Eversley to stem her beloved's thoughts about the earl's manners. "It is time you were looking round for a husband, dear Miranda. You will have no shortage of offers. Have any of those young men proposed to you?"

"I shall never marry," said Miranda violently. "I do not think I am cut out for it. I am only interested in horses. All I want to do is to go back to Melbury Place and breed hunters. Helmslow will run my stud, and I shall settle down to being happy and going hunting once again."

Her aunt ignored her niece's violent tones. "Bravo," she said, as if she entirely approved of this eccentric retreat from the fashionable world. "I own I am not over-fond of horses, myself, but if you dislike society I have no doubt that you might be better back in the country."

"But you will not leave now," asked Mr. Martock in dismay, and in disapproval, too. "The season has not finished and it would seem unforgivably eccentric for a young girl to go home without so much as finishing her first year out. And it would give rise, I fear, to the sort of speculation which might result in the scandal that your aunt so fears. I must say that I think leaving London would be a very bad idea."

"I don't want to stay in London," said Miranda sulkily.

"Well, there is another good reason for staying," said Mr. Martock in his pleasantly firm way. "Your aunt and I hope to be married, and your presence at the wedding is my dearest wish, and hers too, no doubt."

"You must stay for *our* wedding, if not for your

own," put in Lady Eversley. She did not seem to notice the involuntary shudder that shook Miranda at the mention of the word "wedding."

"In the circumstances, I will stay for it," said Miranda. "I suppose I must linger on till the season is over, Mr. Martock, as you say. But I have no heart for it now." She did not offer any explanation of why, but in her own mind she thought how awful it would be to go to parties, and receive no distinguishing attentions from the earl.

"Good, then that's settled, " said her aunt briskly. "Now I must go to Bond Street for I have nothing fit to wear, I swear, and I must buy my trousseau. No doubt you will want to go to your club, James."

Having thus firmly disposed of her lover, Lady Eversley bade Miranda a brief goodbye, and went off in a flurry of excitement, apparently to purchase yards of material and a whole series of new dresses.

Miranda was left alone. It was, she thought, an extremely selfish display from her aunt. Of course, Aunt Dorothy was preoccupied with her coming wedding. It was natural that she should be. But she might have spared a little more time and sympathy for her niece. She felt quite cross with her scatterbrained relative. Lady Dorothy was absurdly pleasure-loving, she thought. It had been quite impossible to talk frankly to her, while Mr. Martock was in the same room. And obviously Lady Eversley was not going to tell him about the letters and the blackmail attempt. But what really hurt Miranda was that she had not stayed, after he had gone, to discuss things more fully with her niece.

Miranda sighed listlessly. The morning seemed to drag interminably. She wondered whether she might not have been happier with a more conventional upbringing. Then, perhaps, she could have filled in the weary empty hours with some needlework, or with practice on the piano. As it was she felt she had no interests to fall back on.

She considered inspecting the stables. At Melbury Place that was always an enjoyable task, which she fulfilled every morning. But here in London, she was not responsible for their smooth running. She had, of course, cast a knowledgeable eye over them and had concluded that though Lady Eversley's head groom knew his horses well enough, his stable management left something to be desired. Miranda could have sworn that the bill for oats and hay was higher than it need be, and that the surplus was probably lining his pockets. It would not be a good idea, though, for her to interfere. Besides, if she went to the stables, she would run up against Helmslow. And he would want to know what his mistress had been up to, taking hackney carriages. Miranda knew from past experience that with a houseful and yardful of servants, nothing remained a secret long.

No, thought Miranda, the stables were out. Nor could she go for a walk in the park. She would need to take a maid or a footman with her, and Miranda had no wish to promenade with a sulky servant dawdling behind. She dared not go alone. She had already taken too many risks in that direction.

Slowly, an hour passed. Miranda occupied herself for at least a quarter of an hour writing a letter to Nanny back in Melbury Place. *I rely on you, dear Nanny, to see that Betty is not teased by the other servants. She had had an unfortunate experience in London, and needs time to recover from it. She is a good girl at heart, I believe, and will prove dutiful and hard-working.* Betty Miller had already been sent off by an early stagecoach, she was relieved to discover that morning. The sooner the girl was away from the temptations of town, the better.

Miranda only wished she could have accompanied her protegée. She longed to be back at Melbury Place, among the familiar places and faces. She was tired of London. *I trust that you and Sellers are in good health,* she wrote. *Helmslow looks after me well here, but I miss you both. In particular, dear Nanny, I miss you.* The letter continued over two sheets in this vein.

But even this occupation could not last forever. So it was with relief that she heard Stratton knock on the door. "A visitor, Miss," was all that he said, and no sooner were the words out of his mouth than the tall figure of the Earl of Templecombe strode in.

"Oh." The abrupt exclamation left Miranda's mouth before she had time to think. Stratton's unusual lapse of duty in not properly announcing the visitor by his name had caught her unawares.

"That is not a very polite way of greeting me, Miss Melbury," said the earl. "Surely you can summon up better manners than that."

But Miranda was in a state of utter confusion. The earl's left shoulder, she noticed, was bandaged and he was carrying his arm in a sling. He looked pale. A wave of sympathy flooded her, and she wanted to beg his forgiveness for leading him into danger. After all, his wound had been got in her service. But somehow the words would not come.

"Thank you, my lord, for calling," she said stiffly. "My aunt is out. She will be desolated at having missed you. She wants to thank you for your help last night to me, and of course, I must take this opportunity of thanking you too."

"I know your aunt is out. That's why I called now," he said impatiently. "But if we are going to banter civilities at each other, Miss Melbury, then I owe you a debt

216

of thanks, too. You undoubtedly saved my life. And I will allow that you are an excellent horsewoman. Not many women that I know could have managed that ride back."

"That is a compliment indeed from a rider like yourself," said Miranda formally. There was a pause, while she gathered her courage in both hands. "I daresay, however, that you may not have perfectly gathered my explanations last night," she said laboriously. "It was not an elopement, you know. Sir Samuel tricked me into joining him in his carriage. I was thrown in the coach by hired ruffians. I know it sounds very unlikely, but it is the truth. I hate Sir Samuel. He is an odious man."

"I know all that," said the earl, and for the first time he smiled directly at her. "When I saw you leave the ballroom, I could not be sure why you had left, and when I saw Sir Samuel's coach disappearing, then I admit I thought it must be an elopement. Directly he took the Dover road, I knew that even if you had joined him willingly, you must have been deceived into thinking he was going to Gretna Green.

"From that moment on, I knew that I was doing the right thing by going in pursuit. I had not really stopped to wonder if I should be interfering. But then when the coach catapulted on its side, I saw my chance and took it."

"I am exceedingly grateful that you did," said Miranda shuddering. "I only wish I could explain everything about Sir Samuel, but I can't."

"I know everything," said the earl for the second time. "Your aunt has just called on me and told me everything. I know all about her indiscreet letters, and Sir Samuel's shocking attempt at blackmail. I even know why I met you rambling round Hyde Park in a very improper way late in the evening."

"Oh. Aunt Dorothy?" asked Miranda, nonplussed. "I thought she had just gone out shopping."

"No," said the earl, smiling. "She had come to tell me everything. I know the truth about the Brasseys. And, incidentally, I know you will be interested to hear that Miss Jennifer Brassey has left London for the north. It seems she has some other relatives there, where she will find a home. So I think we have seen the last of her."

"It is odd, but somehow I felt so sorry for her," said Miranda childishly. "I do not think she was a villain like her cousin, just an unhappy woman. Do you know what has happened to Sir Samuel?"

"I have had word that he, too, has left London for good. His coach proceeded to Dover, it seems, and his household back in London do not expect to see him again. Apparently he left word for the servants to be dismissed and the house to be closed."

"Can we do something about those wretched girls that he has harmed?" asked Miranda. "I know it is perhaps improper to ask, but I do feel that something should be done."

"Do not worry your pretty little head about such things," said the earl, smiling in a way that she found both pleasant and disturbing. "I trust I have persuaded your aunt that she must tell that part of the tale to Mr. Martock's sister. Lady Roehampton is just the person to set inquiries going into things of that nature. I have told your aunt that I will support her, and will vouch for the tale. Lady Roehampton need know nothing of Sir Samuel's blackmailing activities. All she needs to know is about the Floral Street and other establishments. She will not want to know more. There is plenty and enough there for her beloved Society for the Suppression of Vice."

There was a pause. Miranda wondered if she ought

to say something, but the earl's gaze made it difficult for her to think of anything to say.

"Miranda," he said softly. Her name in his mouth sounded completely romantic. "Miranda," he whispered again. "Do you know what your aunt also told me?"

"No," she whispered. She felt very shy.

"She told me that in her honest opinion you were not indifferent to me," said the earl. He looked at her with an intensity that made her eyes fall before his. "Was that true?" he persisted.

"I don't think it was fair of Aunt Dorothy . . ." Somehow Miranda could not bring herself to admit her heart. "Really, I don't think she should have . . ."

Suddenly, she did not exactly know how, she was swept up in a passionate embrace that left her gasping and shaken. The earl's strong arms were round her, and his lips were on hers. His long kiss burned into her very soul, with a fire that Miranda had not before realized existed.

"But, darling your arm . . . be careful," she murmured, alarmed at his strength, when she managed to get her lips free for a second.

"Damn my arm," said the earl briefly, and smothered her protests with a second satisfactory kiss.

It was like Paradise, Miranda thought. Her heart beat faster and stronger than ever before. Her senses swam. It was like nothing before she had ever experienced. Such bliss seemed to flood her inmost being . . . Suddenly a disconcerting thought occurred to her. She burst out laughing.

The earl let go of her. "What the hell is so funny?" he asked scowling, and the sight of his stupefied face made Miranda laugh even more.

"I was just thinking," she said through laughter, "how much nicer love is than hunting. I used to think that there was no greater joy than clearing a four-bar gate . . . don't you see?" She went on, as the earl's face cleared only slowly, "I have discovered something I like better than horses. I love you even better than Diabolo." By now the earl's face was a blank. "He is my black stallion," she explained.

The earl's face broke into a smile. "You adorable little horsewoman," he said, putting his arms safely back around her. "I suppose, coming from you, that is a high compliment. I should have known that you wouldn't be like other women. You are meant to swoon or flush or simper when a gentleman kisses you, not burst into roars of laughter and tell him you like him even better than hunting."

He kissed her passionately for a third time. Then lifting his lips from hers he added: "But I am glad that you do prefer kissing me to hunting."

"Anyway," said Miranda with a saucy smile, looking up to him, "I am sure that gentlemen aren't meant to go round kissing ladies in the abandoned way you do. Why, you kissed me in the curricle, and you were about to kiss me in the park, and now you are kissing me in Lady Eversley's morning room. How improper this all is."

"It is not improper at all. Every gentleman is entitled to kiss the lady he is going to marry," said the earl. "What is more, I have even asked Lady Eversley for permission to pay my addresses."

Miranda emerged from a fourth embrace, her ringlets somewhat ruffled but her spirits soaring. "But you haven't paid your addresses," she said. "You haven't even proposed to me yet."

To her confusion and joy, the earl looked serious for a moment. He relinquished her from his embraces, and with a graceful gesture that amazed her and even frightened her a little, sank onto one knee at her feet. "Darling Miranda," he said, and it was his turn to look up to her, "will you do me the inestimable honor of becoming my wife? There is no other woman I have ever asked that. I love you, I love you so much that I sometimes think I am going mad because of you."

"Yes, please," was all that Miranda could murmur. Large tears fought their way to her eyes, and rolled down her face.

In a flash the earl was on his feet again, holding her firmly in his arms. He had taken his wounded arm out of its sling. "Now, now, sweetheart," he said with a joking tenderness. "Don't take what I said too sadly. Come, come, where is the madcap hoyden I met on the road?"

Looking at him, her eyes swimming with tears, Miranda could manage only a watery smile. "I know I have been a terrible hoyden, and I can't think how on earth you can want to marry me. I never seem to behave right, and I think I shall make a really terrible countess."

"You will make a magnificent countess," said the earl smiling. "Of course, you will have to give up breaking your own horses, and riding like a mad thing on the hunting field. And of course countesses do not spend their time wandering around the stables hobnobbing with grooms."

ABOUT THE AUTHOR

Caroline Courtney

Caroline Courtney was born in India, the youngest daughter
of a British Army Colonel stationed there in the troubled years
after the First World War. Her first husband, a Royal Air
Force pilot, was tragically killed in the closing stages of the
Second World War. She later remarried and now lives with
her second husband, a retired barrister, in a beautiful 17th
century house in Cornwall. They have three children, two
sons and a daughter, all of whom are now married, and four
grandchildren.

On the rare occasions that Caroline Courtney takes time
off from her writing, she enjoys gardening and listening to
music, particularly opera. She is also an avid reader of romantic poetry and has an ever-growing collection of poems
she has composed herself.

Caroline Courtney is destined to be one of this country's
leading romantic novelists. She has written an enormous number of novels over the years—purely for pleasure—and has
never before been interested in seeing them reach publication.
However, at her family's insistence she has now relented, and
Warner Books are proud to be issuing a selection in this uni-
form edition.